FUJINO
OMORI

ILLUSTRATION BY
SUZUHITO
YASUDA

IS it WRONG to TRY to PiCK UP GIRLS iN A DUNGEON?

VOLUME 3

FUJINO OMORI

ILLUSTRATION BY SUZUHITO YASUDA

IS IT WRONG TO TRY TO PICK UP GIRLS
IN A DUNGEON?, Volume 3
FUJINO OMORI

Translation by Andrew Gaippe

DUNGEON NI DEAI WO MOTOMERU
NO WA MACHIGATTEIRUDAROUKA vol. 3
Copyright © 2013 Fujino Omori
Illustrations copyright © 2013 Suzuhito Yasuda
All rights reserved.
Original Japanese edition published in 2013
by SB Creative Corp.
This English edition is published by arrangement
with SB Creative Corp., Tokyo, in care of
Tuttle-Mori Agency, Inc., Tokyo.

English translation © 2015 Hachette Book
Group, Inc.

Yen On
Hachette Book Group
1290 Avenue of the Americas
New York, NY 10104
www.hachettebookgroup.com
www.yenpress.com

Yen On is an imprint of Hachette Book Group, Inc.
The Yen On name and logo are trademarks of
Hachette Book Group, Inc.

The publisher is not responsible for websites (or their
content) that are not owned by the publisher.

First Yen On edition: August 2015

ISBN: 978-0-316-34015-1

10 9 8 7 6 5 4 3 2

RRD-C

Printed in the United States of America

VOLUME 3

FUJINO OMORI
ILLUSTRATION BY **SUZUHITO YASUDA**

PROLOGUE "ALEA JACTA EST"

"Ottar. The boy has gotten stronger."

"Is that desirable, ma'am?"

"Why, yes."

The room was dark. The weak light of dusk filtered in from outside the window.

The corners of Freya's lips curled upward in the flickering light from a single magic-stone lamp sitting on a table.

This was the top floor of Babel Tower, built directly above the Dungeon itself.

There were few furnishings in the room. While that might not have seemed suitable for the highest-class suite in the tower, each individual piece of furniture was beyond lavish. Likewise, every item was placed perfectly within the space to complement everything else.

The décor included a massive bookcase, a bed so big that a normal mind could never have thought of it, and a stylish, dark red carpet. Framing the interior were large murals of the sun and moon.

There, the silver-haired goddess Freya held a wineglass in her hand as she enjoyed a conversation with one of her followers.

"I misjudged him. This isn't simply about status. Just by obtaining magic, the boy's soul now shines even brighter...To my eyes, it looks as if he has been polished."

She held her wineglass up in the cold moonbeam, gazing at the light as it reflected off the lazily sloshing liquid.

The young white wine was crystal clear with no depth. And no flavor either, of course.

But Freya smiled with her silver eyes as she brought the glass to her lips, almost as though she considered that pale color itself to be prized above all else.

"His soul's growth...is it so remarkable?"

"Perhaps so. I wonder," she replied to the stone-faced Ottar as he stood quietly in the corner of the room.

He stood at attention, his eyes on his goddess.

Her silver eyes meeting his rust-colored gaze, Freya slowly and deliberately lowered her eyelids.

"However, there is something…just one thing keeping him from shining through. It's holding him back, like shackles on his soul."

"……"

"Yes, he has enough spirit to shine. Be that as it may, he lacks a strong core. No, he has a good core, but it looks clouded to me…as though something is missing, or blocking it.

"Any ideas, Ottar?" asked Freya over her shoulder, seeking his opinion, as though needing the perspective of another male.

The male animal person, built like a boulder, opened his lips to answer his mistress.

"Perhaps his attachments."

"His attachments…?"

"Yes, it is as you have said, Mistress Freya: the boy's attachments, his connection with the Minotaur…He may not even be aware of it himself, but some part of his past has become a thorn, constantly tormenting him from within."

Ottar knew of Bell's encounter with a Minotaur in the dungeon. While Freya herself didn't exactly hear the story from Bell's mouth, she had gotten enough information to put the story together.

It wasn't much more than a guess, but she was fairly certain that Bell, with that weak body of his, had indeed lost to a Minotaur.

Freya ran a curled finger down the side of her cheek, down to her chin.

"He has some trauma, then…The children really are delicate. We may have a few attachments, but gods are not held back by the past. Very interesting…On the other hand, perhaps you see us as merely whimsical?"

"Don't be absurd."

"If you'd humor me every once in a while, I wouldn't be so bored…"

Ottar's face remained unchanged. "Ah, well…" Freya muttered to herself as she cast her gaze back out the window and onto Bell.

"So tell me, what can we do to free him from these restraints?"

Freya narrowed her eyes as she glanced back at her servant and challenged him with the question.

"A person can only break free from the chains of their past by their own hands. There is no other way."

The ever-stoic Ottar responded directly to his goddess's question.

"…Is that from personal experience?"

"I believe that men are doomed to repeat their own mistakes."

Freya laughed quietly to herself before breaking eye contact.

A cause for concern had just come to light. Freya's good mood carried her deep into thought.

If the shadow of this Minotaur monster is the cause, then the answer is simple: I don't have to do anything, save wait. That boy will grow stronger still and climb over that wall…

With enough time, Bell would become strong enough to defeat a Minotaur.

All he had to do was escape from the past that still had him by the tail. There was no problem to solve.

And the moment he slays the Minotaur, he will shine brighter than ever before…

Once that happened, he would appear before her like a flower in full bloom; one radiant enough to make her fall for him all over again.

She couldn't wait, she admitted to herself. Bell was at the center of her universe now; he had become more appealing to Freya than anything else.

She wanted him, very much.

She wanted him to always be close enough to reach out and touch.

Once her thoughts came to his point, Freya asked Ottar another question.

"Ottar."

"What is it, ma'am?"

"Do you not feel anything? I am becoming entranced with that boy, ignoring all of you already in my *Familia*."

Ottar's face remained unchanged as Freya continued.

"What would you do if that boy becomes stronger than you?"

"......"

"I might treasure him more than you. That place you are standing now might become his."

"As your heart desires, Mistress Freya."

"You wouldn't be jealous?"

Ottar responded with utmost sincerity and trust, without betraying any emotion as he spoke.

"Your love is fair to all. While some may be special, no one is above the rest."

"......"

"Even if you were to dismiss me from this post, I wholeheartedly believe that your love for me will not disappear."

Silver eyes locked with rusty ones.

In the uncomfortable silence that followed, Ottar bent his gargantuan body forward and silently lowered his head.

"I have said too much."

"I don't mind. In fact, quite the opposite. You have become dearer to me."

"Your words bring me great joy."

They casually traded words as though they were so many blows.

Freya let out a conniving laugh as she spun her beautiful voice into her response.

"But it's a shame. You're always so rigid. I would've loved to see you green with envy."

"If that is what you desire."

"...Ha. Hee-hee! Ha-ha-ha! Would you please, Ottar? Please don't make me laugh! If I saw your serious face burn with jealousy, I don't think I could contain myself."

"......"

Freya laughed, seemingly finding the notion truly amusing. She placed the palm of one hand over her mouth and hugged her waist with the other, as though she were a young girl trying to contain herself.

As for Ottar, seeing his goddess like this finally got a reaction out of him, a small twitch of an ear. One of the catlike ears on the top of his head suddenly pointed in a strange direction.

Once Freya had gotten her fill of laughter, she wiped her eyes and turned to face her very embarrassed subordinate to change the subject.

"So Ottar, what do you think?"

"...How do you mean?"

"About the boy. Am I worried over nothing?"

Ottar immediately repaired his posture.

"He will soon become powerful enough to resist me. Powerful enough to break free from these 'attachments' you spoke of."

"......"

"But, part of me is worried if that is well enough. I can't explain it in words...Eventually, it's just a matter of time, before I know it... All of those phrases keep going through my head, and I feel, somehow, timid. I know it's not true, but I feel like I'm in the wrong." Freya whispered under her breath, "Perhaps I'm overthinking it."

It was all she could do to muse, vaguely, that nothing was wrong, and that she had done nothing wrong.

There were no particularly strong grounds for this. But Freya had watched many talented children grow in her *Familia*, and all of them had grown strong given enough time. Surely this boy would follow the same pattern.

At this moment, Ottar squinted his eyes for the first time.

"Ottar, do you think time will solve this problem, too?"

"Yes, indisputably. Given enough time, it will happen. It's just..."

Ottar let his words hang for a moment before speaking with full confidence.

"Those who do not go on adventures will never break out of their shell. That is a fact."

He fell silent.

His true feelings had been revealed.

Somewhere else in Orario, there was a half-elf with the opposite opinion.

These, though, were the words of a man who had survived many close calls—a mature adult who had been forged in the flames of battle. He clearly stated that those who don't go on adventures would never rise past a certain level.

Ottar had pointed out the possibilities of an *unknown* that even Freya couldn't see.

Indeed, it wasn't Freya, but Ottar who saw what the boy could become.

"...I leave his development in your hands, Ottar."

The Goddess of Beauty set the glass of white wine down.

Closing both eyes, it was as if she had turned her back on him.

It was only then that Ottar couldn't hide a hint of suspicion on his face.

"...And what caused this change in the wind?"

"It's it obvious? You now understand the boy better than I do."

Freya's head was down, her voice sounding like that of a pouting child.

She then raised her head, laughing in a very glamorous fashion.

"Enough to make me jealous."

CHAPTER

THE KENKI APPROACHES

The sun was shining down from directly overhead.

Its light brightened the main street north of Babel Tower.

Very few adventurers came up this way; civilians filled the street as well as a certain open café. The seats were occupied by people laughing and enjoying the warmth of the midday sun.

Bell and Lilly sat across from each other at a table surrounded by the parasols of the many patrons enjoying their lunch outside.

"So, you're done with *Soma Familia*?"

"Yes. Because Lilly has no doubt that they think she's dead."

A day had passed since Bell and Lilly made their party anew.

Bell wanted to know about Lilly's current situation, and was listening to her explanation.

"Since Lilly is dead, there is no reason for her to continue being involved in *Soma Familia*. At the same time, *Soma Familia* won't come looking for her. Why would they? Lilly's gone, after all."

Lilly continued, explaining that they shouldn't cause a problem for Bell, either.

Bell's brow darkened slightly as he took in Lilly's face, her clear eyes and charming features now clearly visible thanks to the disappearance of her bangs, which vanished upon her transformation.

"Don't worry about me…Anyway, are you sure you're okay with being labeled as dead?"

"Thank you for your concern, Mr. Bell. But it's better to cut them off. Lilly doesn't have anyone to rely on over there anyway…And as you know, Mr. Bell, Lilly is satisfied with that."

Lilly was speaking from her heart. Bell understood, and decided not to push any further on this topic.

He didn't want to reopen any of the girl's wounds, so he considered the matter resolved.

"I'll take you at your word, Lilly. But I wonder if *Soma Familia* will find out? That you're alive, I mean."

"Lilly can't guarantee that they won't, but she's spent the past two days erasing any trail that could lead to her. There isn't any need to worry. Plus, Lilly has this."

Lilly lightly placed her hands on her head with a small *thud* and rubbed her hair. Her usual chestnut-colored hair shifted to a dark brown as cat ears popped out of her head just behind her hands. Her eyes had become a golden brown.

"*Cinder Ella.*"

Thanks to this magic, Lilly always had an ace up her sleeve. No matter how anyone looked at the girl now, they would see an Animal People child. While the shape of Lilly's face was mostly unchanged, she looked nothing like the prum she really was.

As long as this "ace" was a secret, the chances that anyone else would be able to realize this girl was Lilliluka Erde were one in a million. Bell himself had been shocked when he found out about Lilly's magic.

"Umm, so then…"

"Yes, there's no problem. Even if someone found out, they would never be able to make trouble for you, Mr. Bell."

Bell grimaced and nodded, not worried about his own safety. Yet at the same time, he did feel relieved.

With things how they were, there was almost no way that Lilly would get caught up in another dangerous situation. And even if she were, Bell would be able to help.

Truth be told, Bell felt angry and sad after hearing what Lilly had to say—angry at those who would treat others as if they weren't people, and sad that those who did would go unpunished.

However, thinking about it from Lilly's position, she shouldn't be involved with *Soma Famiila* at all. To do so now would be like calling a pack of wolves onto both Lilly *and* Bell.

As long as Lilly was safe, nothing else mattered. Bell forced his own misgivings out of his mind as he arrived at that conclusion.

They'd already buried the hatchet.

While it wasn't completely gone, the distance between Bell and Lilly had almost disappeared. They were comfortable enough with each other now to reach out and shake hands.

It's a blank slate from today, Bell thought as a smile emerged on his lips.

"......Mr. Bell."

"Eh? What is it?"

"Is this really okay with you, Mr. Bell?"

"Huh?"

"Is it okay to forgive Lilly like this?"

At that moment, Lilly's expression was the exact opposite of Bell's, dark and dispirited.

She looked up at Bell with the eyes of a criminal begging for forgiveness.

"Lilly tricked Mr. Bell. She took advantage of Mr. Bell's kindness and betrayed him."

"......"

"And there's no way to return what Lilly stole. If she's forgiven like this, Lilly'll..."

This was the reason the two couldn't get much closer than a handshake.

Lilly felt horrible. Guilt hung over her head. She craved redemption.

She was tormented by the things she had done in her past. Bell had lost count of how many times she had apologized.

Lilly had lost everything, due to recent events. All of the money and items she carried with her, as well as her life savings of gnome jewels, had been stolen from her by a former "ally" in *Soma Familia.* The knowledge that she had absolutely nothing to give Bell to help make up for what she had taken from him was driving her mad.

No matter how many times Bell told her not to worry about it, rather than cheering up, she looked more and more depressed. It was like she wanted some kind of punishment, something more than just a slap on the wrist.

*But I'm not asking for anything like that...*Bell's face contorted as if he'd just lost an argument. He looked back over the table at Lilly.

He wasn't good at this kind of thing—not just deciding punishment, but even looking down on someone from a moral high ground made Bell uncomfortable.

Up until now, his situation had always been the opposite.

Bell racked his brain, trying to find some way to help alleviate Lilly's feelings of guilt, when reinforcements arrived.

"He-ey! Bell!"

"Ah! Goddess!"

Bell stood up as the voice of a young girl called his name. Just as he expected, the goddess Hestia had arrived at the café.

Hestia wasn't very tall. In fact, she wasn't all that much different from Lilly in terms of height. The goddess wove through the vibrant crowd of customers and made her way to Bell and Lilly's table.

"Sorry to keep you waiting. Have you been here long?"

"No, not at all. I'm the one who should apologize. You had to take time off from your job to come here…"

"Nothing to worry about. So then…this is the girl?"

"Ah, yes. She's the one I told you about…"

"I-I'm Lilliluka Erde. N-nice to meet you." Lilly jumped off the chair and made a quick bow.

The two of them had come to the café today at Hestia's request.

Her intentions were clear. She wanted to see with her own eyes the supporter working with the only member of her *Familia*.

If Lilly didn't receive Hestia's permission, their newly reformed party could be disbanded before it even got started. Knowing that was a very real possibility, Lilly couldn't hide her nervousness as she looked up to face the goddess.

Sensing the tension, a small "ah" escaped Bell's lips as if he suddenly remembered something important.

"Oh no. I forgot to get a chair for you, Goddess…"

"……! What, it's nothing to worry about! With this many people, I doubt there's a spare chair anyway. Go ahead and have a seat, Bell. I'll sit on your knee!"

"Ha-ha-ha, you sure like joking around like that, don't you,

Goddess? Just wait here for a minute. I'll go find someone and get another chair ready."

He left with a big smile on his face. It was the innocent smile of a child who knew nothing of plots and schemes.

Hestia turned and watched him leave, standing still for a moment before her twin black ponytails sunk like the tail of a sad puppy.

Lilly looked on in confusion at the dark cloud of sadness hovering over Hestia.

"...Wh-what luck. I wanted to find a way to get him to go away for a moment anyway. It's no big deal."

"Y-yes."

Hestia plunked her rear end into Bell's now vacant chair, her face pouty and a bit red.

Lilly followed suit and sat down.

"Well, let's get right to it. Never know when he'll be back. No need for introductions, right? I'm sure Bell told you who I am."

"Y-yes."

It would still be a few more minutes before Lilly realized in what direction Hestia was driving the conversation.

While Lilly was a young prum girl, her youthful look and innocence were nothing compared to Hestia's. The goddess seemed to exist right on the border between "fetching girl" and "lovely young lady."

But that uncertainty somehow only accentuated her beautiful, fine features.

She was part mischievous troublemaker, but also refined—both elements seemingly intertwined within her.

Sunlight that managed to find its way between the parasols struck Hestia's jet-black ponytails, making them glitter around her.

"I'll ask you up front. Supporter, are you still trying to run any scams?"

"—"

Lilly was taken aback by the too-direct question.

Hestia didn't even blink as she stared across the table. Despite her looks, Hestia possessed a dignity befitting a goddess.

Lilly suddenly realized she was being tested. Hestia had seen right through her.

As proof, Hestia had not said Lilly's name even once up to this point. However, after all that Lilly had done to Bell, it was only natural that the goddess saw her as an untrustworthy prum.

In response, Lilly spoke earnestly from her heart. "Absolutely not. Lilly was saved by Mr. Bell. Lilly doesn't want to do anything that could hurt or betray him anymore."

Their eyes met, both unblinking. Neither looked away. The background noises of the street and the café seemed distant.

No one can lie to a god. While she had heard the words before, it was not until that moment that Lilly realized how true they were. Hestia could see right through her.

The gods and goddesses had the power to detect any lie here in the earthly world of Gekai, if they felt like it.

"…Hmm, okay. I'll believe those words."

Hestia's words put a merciful end to an extremely long minute for Lilly.

All of the air that had built up in Lilly's lungs was suddenly released as the muscles in her shoulders relaxed.

"Supporter, Bell is a very special person to me. He's my pride and joy, the center of my world. My first member, my first family. I can tell you honestly that I don't want to lose him."

Hestia paused for a moment, inhaling, and then continued.

"Bell has told me a lot about you, including your motivations for stealing."

"……"

"I have no intention of giving you any cheap sympathy. In fact, that would be impossible. So, I have nothing to say on the subject… However."

She let the word hang to let Lilly know that this was the important part.

As she opened her mouth to speak again, Hestia's eyes blocked out everything except for the girl.

"If you should do something, *anything*, that puts that boy in a dangerous situation again…I will make you pay."

—Lilly couldn't move.

For a moment, she forgot how to breathe.

A very important fact had slipped her mind. While the girl in front of her didn't look much different from anyone else around them, she was from a completely different world. She was a goddess.

It was so obvious that Hestia had the power—like all deities from Deusdia—to turn this entire city to ash in an instant, that Lilly had forgotten it.

Under a blue gaze so cold it sent icicles through her heart, Lilly drew power from her true feelings to make a response. It took all of her might to open her mouth to speak.

"…Lilly swears to you. She will never do anything to put Mr. Bell in danger, Lady Hestia in danger…or even Lilly herself, ever again."

Other café patrons continued their casual conversations with no idea what was unfolding behind them.

The two of them sat there in silence for some time before Hestia closed her eyes, signaling the end of that conversation.

Blinking several times, Hestia mouthed, "Okay" to the girl. Seeing that broke the ice that had kept Lilly's body rigid, and she went limp. She was about to fall face-first into the table but managed to catch herself at the last moment.

After delivering her warning, Hestia crossed her arms in front of her incredibly bulbous chest and eyed Lilly silently. She started sulking. Lilly noticed the heavy aura emanating from the goddess and did everything she could to make her body smaller.

"…Supporter. I'll be honest with you."

"Y-yes?"

"I hate you. I don't want you anywhere near Bell."

"!"

Lilly's eyes shot open as Hestia continued.

"It should be obvious. I knew you were bad news from the moment I first heard about you—taking advantage of Bell's kindness and doing whatever you please. Even now, you're trying to gain favor by acting like you've already paid your dues. What's your scheme, you deceiving vixen?!"

The cat ears on top of Lilly's head from her "Cinder Ella" magic began to shake. The prum then broke out in a cold sweat, confused by Hestia's choice of words.

"Besides, what's *with* you? You've been making that downcast face ever since I sat down. I'm getting depressed just looking at you!"

It was like she was claiming Lilly's very presence made the food taste bad.

The goddess kept going, pouting like a toddler.

"I'll bet you were thinking about Bell, weren't you?"

"!"

"How did I know, you ask? Because I saw a look on your face that I only see when I look in the mirror! Ahhh, I hate this! I don't want you spending time with Bell!"

Terrible waves of dread began to run up Hestia's back.

The other patrons had noticed something was going on, their eyes on the two girls but inching away. Lilly looked like she was going to cry.

"Being saved by Bell made you turn over a new leaf, huh? Did you stop to think that you're just going to cause him more trouble because he's too kind for his own good?"

"?!"

"He won't do anything to you for revenge, so you're feeling the crushing weight of guilt on your shoulders. But if I may say so, you're just taking advantage of him. I really, really hate you."

Hestia's words were blades, cutting deeper and deeper.

Hestia's eyes locked squarely on the prum. Lilly couldn't make a sound.

"Fine, then. I'll punish you in Bell's place. But just so you know, you have no right to refuse. I'll give a pure 'Judgment' right here and now."

Air shot of out Hestia's nose in a flow of anger.

A dazzled Lilly could do nothing more than nod. There might even have been a part of her that accepted the words of Bell's goddess and wanted to go along with them.

Lilly waited for Hestia's mouth to open again, every nerve in her body about to explode.

As for Hestia, she was grinding her teeth together, menacingly towering over Lilly...until words failed her. Hestia let out a deep sigh.

"Please, look after Bell."

"...eh?"

"Tch." Hestia almost spat the sound in Lilly's direction. "Let me just say this: I'm not doing it for you. After hearing him talk about you, I'm worried about Bell. You could say my fears were confirmed... He's easily tricked."

"......"

"So I ask you. Make sure he doesn't get fooled by some stranger. You must guard him."

Lilly sat there in shock. She gathered her thoughts, trying to respond, but nothing came out of her mouth.

Hestia's gaze didn't allow it.

"You know, I'm not doing something cheeky like passing judgment on you, right? We deities don't do that nowadays. The reason you feel guilty is because you won't forgive yourself."

Hestia intensified her glare, as if to say *Don't go to Bell looking for forgiveness.*

"If you want to pay him back, help him until he's satisfied. It's obvious. You know that thing called sincerity? And finishing what you start? If you really have changed, then prove it with your actions."

Hestia's torrent of words finally came to an end.

Hestia may have been harsh, but Lilly could sense the goddess's true colors.

The Goddess Hestia had given her a chance. She was merciful.

She was generous and noble at the same time.

Everything up to that point had been her personal feelings. But despite all that, she decided to allow Lilly to be Bell's supporter.

She would extend mercy to anyone; she was a protector of those in need.

Thankful for her sudden warmth, Lilly silently looked up at Hestia before giving her a deep bow of her head.

The aura between the two girls had become as tranquil as a lagoon hidden deep within a forest.

"Sorry to keep you waiting—!"

"...I grant you my blessing to work with him. Please be sure to protect him. Just don't do anything more than that."

"Wha...?"

Hestia's sudden warning broke the tranquility. Lilly's eyes opened in disbelief.

Before she could ask her what she meant by that, Bell set a chair down at their table. The moment he opened his mouth to apologize yet again, Hestia quickly reached out, snagged his arm, and pulled it into her.

"Ah—"

"Goddess...?"

"Shall we reintroduce ourselves? Nice to meet you, Supporter. Looks like you're going to be helping *my* Bell out a lot in the near future."

Hestia put a little too much emphasis on "my." Her aura had changed once again. Now she was like a tigress protecting her territory. Her cold stare from before had become a line of fire, as if to say *hands off or I'll tear you apart.*

Lilly flinched away, her cheek twitching at Hestia's maneuvering.

She was a goddess. Generous and righteous, Hestia was worthy of worship and praise.

But she was also a child.

Or rather—a rival.

She was pulling Bell's arm up against her, purposefully creating a barrier in front of him. A spark of anger flashed in the back of Lilly's mind.

They had come to a point of peace just a moment ago, but this was different.

Whoosh! Lilly reached out with both hands and grabbed ahold of Bell's other arm.

Lilly faced down Hestia's burning glare of death with her own defiant gaze.

"No no, the pleasure's all Lilly's. Bell has always been *so terribly kind* to Lilly, after all."

"......!"

A young prum on one side, a young goddess on the other.

They might have looked like cute little girls on the outside, but they stared each other down with the faces of fully-grown women.

Not even tall enough for their legs to touch the ground sitting in their chairs, the two young ladies glared knives at one another.

G-Goddess—?!

Bell's arm was being pressed into Hestia's rather extensive cleavage and he was starting to panic. He had no idea what was taking place just under his chin.

In the battle of the two ladies, the goddess had claimed the first point.

"D-drat...! Just like a goddess...So those things aren't just for show...!"

"Did you say something, Supporter...?"

"Um, Lilly. What're you planning to do next...?" After the smoke had cleared, Bell struck up a conversation.

Everyone had calmed down to the point that they were sitting peacefully in their chairs. Lilly's eyes, currently a golden brown hue, looked at Bell in confusion.

"You don't exactly...have a home to go back to right now, do you, Lilly?"

"No, I don't. That was true before, too, but Lilly's staying at cheap motels."

Lilly flashed a nervous smile as Bell turned his attention to Hestia.

Although Hestia's lip twitched ever so slightly, she made eye contact and gave a big nod.

"Lilly, if it's okay with you...Why don't you stay with us at our home?"

© Suzuhito
Yasuda

"...?"

"What I'm trying to say is, do you want to join *Hestia Familia*? It's just me and the goddess right now."

Of course Bell knew that Lilly was already a member of *Soma Familia*, but he also knew that she had no connection with them anymore.

That's why he thought he'd make the offer. Rather than leave her out on the streets, why not invite her to join them? It was something that Bell himself wanted, too.

Hestia showed little reaction, and all that was left was for Lilly to agree.

"...Lady Hestia, is that okay? You don't hate Lilly...?"

"Hee-hee-hee...Don't get the wrong idea. No matter how much I don't like you, ignoring a child in your situation goes against my principles. I came here today knowing that I might end up hosting you until you find your next job."

Hestia's cheeks were turning red as she braced every muscle in her head to squeeze out those words with a straight face. Her obvious lie made Bell grimace uncomfortably.

Lilly chuckled at the two of them before taking a deep breath and slowly shaking her head.

"Thank you, Mr. Bell, Lady Hestia. But the thought alone is enough for Lilly."

"Wha...Wh-why?!"

"Lilly would feel bad for taking advantage of your kindness again, and...Lilly is still a member of *Soma Familia*."

Laughing at Bell's stunned reaction, Lilly reached around her back from over her shoulder.

Even Hestia squinted her eyes, thinking about the status engraved at the tips of Lilly's fingers.

"As a member of *Soma Familia*, Lilly isn't allowed to go to Mr. Bell and Lady Hestia's home. If the fact that Lilly was staying there were found out, it would cause trouble for both of you. Lilly couldn't forgive herself if that happened."

"I-I'm not worried about that...Oh." Bell was just about to take a bite out of his lunch when he suddenly realized something important and froze.

This was no longer just his problem. His family would be in danger as well.

Bell closed his eyes as though a sudden headache had struck him. Forcing his eyelids half-open, he looked over at Hestia.

"Supporter, what are the conditions for leaving *Soma Familia*? Is it forbidden altogether? What did your god say about it?"

"Soma has never said anything directly...But most likely, Lilly thinks it involves a large amount of money."

"Money, huh..."

Besides members, the main thing that *Hestia Familia* lacked was money.

Thanks to Bell's efforts in the Dungeon, the two of them were much better off now than they had been a month ago, but they still had to save as much as possible. The most money they could hope to offer at this point would be around 10,000 vals.

And even if by some miracle Bell and Hestia were able to raise enough money to pay for Lilly's release, there was no way that Lilly would be willing to accept it.

"Is it that difficult to break away from a *Familia*...? I know someone who has..."

"It's up to the god. Some will listen to that kind of request, others won't."

The risk of leaving a *Familia* was all on the person leaving; it was also hazardous to the *Familia* itself. The biggest risk was, of course, information being leaked.

No matter how dissolute the god or goddess was, this level of *Familia* management needed to be handled very delicately. Generally speaking, deities preferred to avoid their members leaving the group.

"The person you're talking about might have circumstances that they can't discuss." Hestia spoke to Bell after a quick glance at Lilly. Both Bell and the prum understood what she was getting at.

Lilly still belonged to the same *Familia*, but at the same time was separate. She was no different from a street cat, a stray adventurer.

As for the person who had received permission to leave their *Familia*—Mama Mia, the owner of The Benevolent Mistress—Bell had a feeling that Hestia was right. Considering a few things that Syr Flover and the others had let slip in conversation, it's very possible Mia might have some "special circumstances."

Even without asking directly, Bell was getting a good sense of just how difficult life was for people who left their *Familia*.

"...What about people who didn't choose to be a part of the *Familia*? They don't have a say it in it?"

"A child is part of the family. Farmer's children become farmers. That's how it is, Mr. Bell."

If a child's parents were already members of a *Familia*, that child was destined to join, whether they liked it or not.

Looking at it from the god's or goddess's perspective, the child was the parent's responsibility. It wasn't as though the god had asked to have a crying baby in their home, so they weren't likely to take care of it.

To be blunt, it wasn't the god's concern.

In the end, permission to leave a *Familia* came down to the god's disposition. Did they have a generous streak, or not?

Because if the member was unlucky, they could be asked for an unreasonably large sum of money, or be given an impossible task to complete as their god watched from a distance, enjoying the show.

Bell looked over at the smiling Lilly with concern in his eyes.

"Without Soma's assistance, you can't update your status...and I suppose you can't covert."

"Probably not..."

"But you're not planning to stay at this level forever, right? Are you planning to pay him a visit at some point?"

"Yes. Lilly knows it's not an option right now, but Lilly will go to Soma when the time is right. Lilly's not sure if he'll listen to her, though..."

With Lilly's words, the conversation came to a sudden end. The three of them sat in their chairs, deep in thought.

Amid this thick but delicate silence, Bell raised his head to ask

Lilly a question. "Well then, what are you going to do, Lilly? Stay by yourself in some room again…?"

"Actually, there is an old gnome that knows Lilly well…Not *Lilly* Lilly, but close enough. Anyway, he should be willing to give Lilly a hand. Lilly's planning to stay at his shop for the time being. Ah, of course she'll be working! She'll do her best not to use her magic and to do honest work."

Bell heard no waver in her voice. The knowledge that Lilly had a plan in mind made him feel a little better.

I think I should talk to Eina again…

It was difficult to think about, but Bell couldn't see any way for the *Soma Familia* situation to be solved without Eina Tulle's help.

It was the Guild's policy not to get involved with problems concerning *Familias* unless something major was taking place.

As the organization that makes Orario tick, the Guild didn't have time to worry about the misfortune of individual adventurers and supporters.

Their role of "support" only involved teaching the adventurers and supporters ways to harvest magic stones more effectively. They didn't typically listen to personal issues.

Bell held his temple with one hand as he realized he had been spoiled by Eina's kindness.

"Hey, hey, are you sure it's all right, forcing yourself on some poor old guy like that? I could introduce you to the manager at my job, you know," said Hestia.

"No, no. Lilly doesn't want to be around when someone forgets how to use a magic-stone stove and blows the whole stand sky-high. Thanks for the offer, but Lilly politely refuses."

"How do you know about that?!"

"Stories about the Loli goddess's curse and the disaster on North Main are quite famous in this neighborhood, so…"

"Eeeeeeek!!!! Not in front of Beeeeeellll!!!!"

"Mmmmph?!"

At any rate, thought Bell, *as long as they're willing to put up with my white-haired head, I'll bow to the girls laughing in front of me any day.*

Finally seeing honest laughter coming from Lilly for the first time was infectious, and he broke into a smile himself.

I make my way at a brisk pace down Northwest Main: "Adventurers Way."

I've said good-bye to the goddess and Lilly, and am *en route* to the Guild headquarters. I can't shake the feeling that I need to at least let Eina know about *Soma Familia*, and other details of the conversation we just had.

The shops lining the street are already open, every one of them busy and lively.

Since adventurers travel this street daily, the shops in this area do their best to stand out with their building design. That accessory shop over there has a waterfall of ale running down the sides of the entrance for decoration, and the item shop next to it is built from ash-colored bricks that look solid as iron. Every shop window has its highest-quality items lined up and on display.

I wonder if most adventurers are taking the day off, as there are a ton of tough-looking demi-humans in street clothes out shopping right now. Most of them are in small groups, like they're in the same party, milling around together as they chatter about this and that topic, laughing often.

That would be so nice. Always being with a group of friends who know you better than anyone else, fighting for each other, even shopping together...Honestly, I'm a little jealous.

Ah, there it is. A massive temple on the side of the road, a pantheon.

I walk through the front garden and between the white marble pillars of the Guild headquarters.

It's just past noon, and most adventurers are in the Dungeon by now so the lobby is mostly empty. The sheer whiteness of the massive hall really stands out when almost no one is here. Without the usual crowd of fellow adventurers blocking my vision, I find Eina almost instantly.

"......?"

She's got a customer at her window.

A single adventurer, standing across the counter from Eina, is holding something wrapped in a white cloth.

Eina's nodding. She looks troubled somehow, like they're talking about something serious. I'm so focused on Eina's expression that I don't even glance at the adventurer, whose back is to me as I carefully walk up to the counter for a closer look. But out of the corner of my eye, I notice the long blond hair and sleek, feminine features.

Eina notices my presence when I'm just a few meders away. Her emerald-green eyes shoot open in surprise.

That starts a chain reaction.

The person at the counter slowly turns to face me.

Wha—

From beneath swaying golden locks appear two golden eyes.

A soft, rounded chin, and thin neck. Even if I hadn't noticed her milky white, smooth skin, she would've still struck me as beautiful.

There's a slight look of surprise, seeing me standing here, on a face so gorgeous that it's on par with the goddesses themselves.

Miss Aiz Wallenstein.

I forget to breathe as the three of us just stand there, a triangle of surprised silence.

"..."

"..."

"..."

My gaze is locked firmly with Aiz's, but I can see Eina's eyes jumping back and forth between us as well.

Now I can't breathe at all. All I can see are those golden eyes, my mind completely blank.

The silence continues.

Keeping my face unchanged, I force my right leg backward and slowly turn my body away from her.

The moment I hear one of them say, "Huh?" I make a break for the door. Every fiber of my being wants out, now!

"B-Bell! Wait!"

I ignore Eina's voice echoing after me, just running, running, running.

My feet pound on the white marble floor, my arms pumping so hard that my shirt might catch fire. Almost out the door!

—Why the heck would Eina be talking to *her*?!

—What the hell is going on?!

This can't be good. I shake my head to get all the images of bad things that might happen to me out of my mind. My instincts lead me out of the lobby, my ears burning red as I put on speed.

Breaking through the confusion outside the front door, I blaze through the front garden and dash toward the safety of the crowded street.

But at that moment, I feel a sudden burst of wind from behind me.

Suddenly, she's standing between me and the street, her blond hair flowing in the breeze she created when she ran past me.

"—DAHH?!"

I see her, but I'm going full speed. There's no way I can avoid slamming right into her, and I watch every horrifying second of it in slow motion through my wide-open eyes.

"Bell? Miss Wallenstein?!"

I clench my eyes tight just before impact, but I can hear Eina's footsteps as she comes out of the Guild…Wait, where's the impact?

I carefully open my eyes only to see a thin arm wrapped around my stomach. Another is supporting my back. She is holding me…

I look up a little higher. She's looking down on me, her eyebrows low.

"…Sorry. Are you okay?"

"—I'M S-SORRY!!"

My face bright red, I practically jump out of her arms.

I take a moment to collect myself, and the sudden jolt of seeing her starts to fade away. It seemed that I'd been…held.

"What do you think you're doing?! Running off like that when someone is trying to talk to you is very rude, I'll have you know!"

"I'm s-sorry, Miss Eina…"

I apologize to a very angry Eina out of reflex, but my eyes are drawn to Miss Wallenstein.

The moment her gaze meets mine, I quickly look away and ask Eina a question.

"S-so what is all this...? Why are you...and you...?!"

"Ah...Miss Wallenstein wanted to talk with you, Bell."

"Huh?!"

Eina heaves a sigh at my total lack of understanding, and tells me nothing more.

My eyes snap back to Miss Wallenstein as she takes the white cloth off the thing she's holding.

An emerald-green vambrace emerges.

I don't think my eyes have ever opened wider than they do at that moment.

"She found this in the Dungeon and wanted to give it back to you personally. She came to me to ask to set up a meeting with you."

She speaks with a matter-of-fact tone, like it should have been obvious. As for me, I'm still in shock.

Three days ago, I fought against wave after wave of monsters on the tenth level of the Dungeon. It got knocked off my arm in the chaos, but I'd been so focused on catching up to Lilly that I didn't take the time to retrieve it...

That's when it hits me. The mysterious adventurer who cleared a path for me, protected me...was *her*.

"...Bell. I'll leave the two of you alone to talk."

"Huh?!"

My shoulders spin violently in Eina's direction as soon as her words hit my ears.

Screaming silently under my breath, I make one last plea to her.

"W-wait, Miss Eina! I'm begging you, please stay here with me...! I—I'm dying here!"

"You're a young man, aren't you? There are many things that need to be said, so man up and say them, all right?" She gives me a quick nod and mouths, "Good luck."

Eina is probably just trying to be nice and give us some privacy, but the thought of being alone with *her* is enough to make me cry. Eina turns on her heel and goes back into the Guild. Suddenly I understand how a puppy feels as it's abandoned in a box by the side of the road and watches its master get smaller in the distance.

"…Umm, here."

"!"

Hearing her voice makes me spin around and take the vambrace from Miss Wallenstein in one movement.

She's almost my height; barely tall enough to look me in the eyes. And she's staring right at me.

My whole body has to be red by this point. My mouth is shut tight.

"I apologize."

"Huh…?"

"It was my fault that that Minotaur wasn't slain, and caused you so much trouble and injury…I have been hoping for a chance to apologize since then. I am very sorry."

I can't believe my ears *or* my eyes, as she lowers her head in a light bow. Getting a grip on the situation, I force my mouth open and drive the words out.

"N-no, no! It was all my fault for going down to the fifth level in the first place! You've done nothing wrong, Miss Wallenstein! Actually, you're my savior! I'm the one who should be apologizing to you, I'm the idiot who turned cocky and got run around in circles…S-sorry!"

Shaking from head to toe, everything that I have to say suddenly comes spilling out of my mouth at once.

After all that I've been through—every time she's saved my life— to have her apologize to me makes me want to disappear off the face of the earth out of embarrassment.

"Well, um, what I'm trying to say…"

I think my face is going to melt from how fast I'm racking my brain for the right words to express what I've wanted to say for so long—until finally they come:

"For all the times you've rescued me…THANK YOU SO MUCH!"

I bow as low as I can without face-planting into the street.

I can see the stone blocks of the road as a bead of sweat rolls down my nose and drops to the ground.

The sounds of the people in the street around me seem distant, drowned out by the thumping drum in my chest.

Neither of us moves for several seconds.

I finally work up the courage to look up and straighten my back.

Miss Wallenstein is just calmly standing there, with the slightest hint of a smile on her lips.

"—!"

Kaaahhhh...Air escapes from my lungs again as a new wave of embarrassment shoots through my body.

I lower my chin, hiding her smile behind my bangs.

Even the butterflies in my stomach are blushing at this point.

"..."

"..."

No one says a word.

As the two of us stand in silence, the only thing moving is time.

This is a bridge that all adventurers and normal people alike must cross. But all I'm able to do in the spacious front garden of the Guild is stand there, unable to make a sound.

"You're doing well...in the Dungeon?"

"Y-yes!"

She breaks the silence, and I respond as quickly as I can.

She continues talking, her facial expression almost void of emotion.

"Looks like you can make it down to the tenth level now...That's impressive."

"No, not at all! I've only gotten that far because I have help! I've still got a long way to go! I haven't even come close to reaching my goal yet...!"

Being complimented by my idol out of the blue like that is too much to handle. Here comes a new wave of panic!

My hands fly up, shaking back and forth while my eyes spin.

"I mean, when I fight monsters in the Dungeon, I'm just winging it like a total amateur. I don't know how many times a monster's almost gotten me. I know I have to get stronger, but I'm still just so weak and I don't feel like I'm getting better at all, well, um...?!"

My nerves are squeezing words out of me at a rate I've never felt before. At this point, I don't know if I'm trying to sound humble or modest or what.

"..."

Miss Wallenstein just stands there, staring silently at the panicked mess that's trying to talk to her: me.

Finally, she moves. She reaches up slowly with one hand and strokes her chin, as if thinking about something.

It takes me a few seconds to notice because I can't see straight, but I gain my bearings long enough to ask her a question.

"Ah...um, is something wrong?"

She doesn't respond right away. Instead, a look of uncertainty passes over her face as she throws a punch at the air between us. She holds that pose for a few more silent moments.

A look of nervousness overtakes her face before she opens her mouth to speak.

"Shall I...teach you how?"

"...Huh?"

"...How to fight. You don't have anyone to teach you, am I right?"

It takes me quite a while to understand what she is asking.

My eyes open wide; I feel like I'm going insane.

"W-why...why would you offer something like that...?!"

"...Because you look like you want to get stronger, I think. I understand that feeling," says Miss Wallenstein, adding something about it being a way to pay me back for the trouble I went through.

How can she be so calm?! It feels like my head is about to explode!

I can learn how to fight? From her? The very person who I want to catch up to will teach me?

Is that okay?

Am I understanding this correctly? It's not a mistake?

I'm still nothing compared to her, and yet I have a chance to learn by her hand? Even physically touch her?

But then there's the problem with her being in a different *Familia*.

My mind spins with questions, but they're no more than an attempt to hide my true feelings.

I want to talk to, know about, and spend time with her.

Just thinking about it makes me feel crazy, but the deepest place in my heart wants nothing more than an opportunity to be together with her.

As all the thoughts swirling around with me are about to tear me apart, I think about the obvious answer and try to string the words into a response.

"…"

Aiz watched in silence as a very flustered Bell tried to collect his thoughts.

There were no lies in what Aiz had said to Bell a moment ago. She could hear his earnest desire to get stronger, and she could relate to him. That was reality.

But of course, she didn't make the offer out of pure good will. There was something she wanted to know.

The first hint of something different was the silverback.

Then it was the fact he'd made it down to the tenth level.

Aiz had seen this boy pull off one miracle after another, witnessing an unbelievable amount of growth in his skills and abilities in a very short amount of time.

The raw newbie she happened to run into during the Minotaur incident had improved enough to draw her interest.

How'd he do it…?

She wanted to know the secret of his growth. Study it.

For herself.

This was a major reason why she'd offered to train him.

"I don't know what you could do with how I am now…but if you're going to offer…"

"…"

At the same time, she felt a bit guilty.

The boy believed that her suggestion was based on pure generosity. Hiding her true motives from him made her heart twinge.

Bell held his head as he spoke, words once again leaking out of him mouth as Aiz calmly watched.

She grabbed the hilt of the sword at her waist as a way of cutting through her own misgivings.

"...U-um, Miss Wallen...stein..."

The boy looked up.

His face was still red, making his stark white hair more intense than usual. But his eyes were focused as he looked into hers, before throwing his body into a deep bow.

"I will learn everything you are willing to teach!"

At last, a strong response.

Looking at the resolve in his eyes, Aiz promised herself that as a way to apologize for her true motives, she would do everything in her power to meet his expectations.

"...Very well. I will do my best."

CHAPTER 2

OX AND HARE SPECIAL TRAINING

The sky is covered in darkness.

The sun hasn't yet risen in the eastern sky, but the horizon is beginning to lighten. It's that moment before dawn when you're not sure if it's night or morning.

The city wall...I've never been up here before.

I woke up much earlier than normal this morning and climbed up to the top of the wall encircling the city of Orario.

I'm standing on the northwest edge. Looking back inside over the city, the view is absolutely breathtaking.

I can see the Pantheon, the Coliseum, buildings that are probably home to large *Familias*, and other tall structures all at once. Even from this distance, I can make out the minute details of the craftsmanship on each of them. Color me impressed!

But of course, there's one that stands out above all the rest in the center of the city: Babel Tower. Its sheer presence is almost overwhelming. Add in the little houses filling the city blocks, and I know I will never get tired of standing here.

Looking up and down the main streets that separate Orario into eight pieces, most buildings' lights are dim. It's almost like the clamor of the city is quieting. One by one, specks of light go out as magic lamps are being shut off all over the place.

And to think, I actually live in this metropolis! Shivers go down my spine and my heart beats faster with excitement every time I remember where I am.

"Are you prepared?"

"Ah, y-yes!"

Her voice ringing like a bell in my ears, I turn around to face Miss Wallenstein.

She's the reason I'm here right now. I'm going to learn how to fight.

She said that her *Familia*, *Loki Familia*, is going on an expedition in a few days. So we don't have much time, but she'll work with me until she leaves. That's why we decided yesterday to start training today.

"Sorry to make you come all the way out here…"

"D-don't worry! It's not a problem!"

Being a member of *Loki Familia*, this is something she isn't supposed to do. If another member of her *Familia* finds out that she's training a member of a different group in combat techniques, there will be major problems for sure.

That's why we've come all the way to the top of the wall—to stay out of sight.

Thinking about it from her position, staying hidden and only meeting occasionally is the only option.

As for why we're here so early, I need to go into the Dungeon like normal to make money. So rather than train after a hard day's work, it makes more sense to do this first.

"Well, um, Miss Wallenstein, what should I…"

"…Aiz."

"Huh?"

"Call me Aiz."

The second I realize she's telling me how to address her, I nearly fall over backward.

"Everyone calls me that. Does it make you uncomfortable?"

"Eh, erm, um……No, I'm comfortable with that."

Why would I refuse? I say to myself with my hand over my mouth. Something in her voice sounds like she'll be disappointed if I don't call her by her first name.

My cheeks flush red. Of course, there hasn't been much time when I've stood in front of Miss Wallenstein…er, *Aiz*, and not been bright red…

Anyway, hopefully I've been able to convey some impression of how strange this situation is.

"…A-Aiz, what should I do now?"

"…A good question."

"Huh?"

Her voice is slightly heavy; how should I react to that?

Aiz's eyebrows fall as she puts a hand to her delicate chin. She looks like she's trying to squeeze an idea out of her brain.

"I've been thinking very hard…since yesterday."

Her head snaps the other way as if her neck is on a spring, like a child being scolded.

Where's all the grace and refinement she's always had?

This is…strange.

My idol, my Aiz Wallenstein, and the real person are drifting apart…

"…Can you show me your form?"

"Y-yes, sure."

I do what she said, working a light sweat in the process.

Taking my dagger out, and feeling a bit embarrassed, I take two or three swipes at the air beside me as she watches.

She just stares at me, eyes following me intently.

"Do you only use your knife?"

"Eh……?"

"The knife wielders I know use kicks and martial arts to fight."

Come to think of it, she's right. When fighting in the Dungeon, I rely completely on my weapon. I can count on one hand the number of times I've kicked or punched a monster.

I look down at my limbs for a moment before Aiz says, "Give it to me," and takes the weapon out of my hand.

She strikes a pose; I guess she's going to show me an example?

"…Like this."

She's holding the dagger backward in her right hand, the blade coming out from behind her pinkie, and her left knee is forward, foot hovering just above the ground.

With her knee in midair, Aiz tilts her head to the side.

She puts her leg back down, and lifts it up one more time…again tilting her head to the side.

"…?"

"…"

Aiz lifts and lowers her knee over and over, and each time she tilts her head.

At this point, I can't hide my sweat or my confusion. It feels really awkward, watching her like this. But she's giving me an example to follow. I should watch as closely as I can.

Does she just...not have a clue...?

"Hm—"

—Was my last thought.

Aiz's body suddenly blurred, as though she'd taken hold of something.

"—Huh?"

Using her right leg to jump into the air with a *smack*, her whole body spins.

Completely ignoring the stunned sounds coming out of my mouth, she extends her left leg, tracing an arc around her in the air.

Her miniskirt flutters; dark blue leggings up to her knees flash before my eyes.

The instant her pale-white inner thigh flashes in front of my eyes—I'm launched skyward.

"Ah—"

A high-speed spinning jump kick.

I'd been too close to the frighteningly fast kick of a top-class adventurer. I both see it and don't as her foot hits me square in the chest and sends me flying toward the edge of the city wall.

I can't react, can't defend, can't even scream, as my body slams into the stone barrier with incredible force, my outstretched arms and legs hitting hard enough to leave a full-body imprint behind as I collapse to the floor.

What the hell was that?!

She kicked me right out of my own body.

It takes all the strength I have left to lift my head up enough to get a look at Aiz. Her face is expressionless as always, but it looks like this time her eyes are a bit wider as she stares down at me.

...Yep, she's clueless...

The last of my strength gone, I manage to arrive at that one realization before I pass out.

"Sorry..."

I'm only out for a few seconds. I wake up to Aiz's apology and a sad look on her face.

I do my best to force a smile and tell her not to worry about it, but my chest is in pain and I think I'm choking on my collarbone.

After that, we try a few more times through trial and error, but nothing feels like it's working.

Seeing her face deep in thought after every failure, it feels like I might need to make a rather uncomfortable exit.

Under a sky still waiting for sunrise, a very heavy mood descends onto both of us.

"...Enough. Let us fight."

"Huh?!"

She's been silent for I don't know how long, before her head snaps up and she speaks to me.

She stands, her hand firmly grasping the hilt of her sword.

I jump in surprise as she draws her sword and sets it down next to the barrier. Then she turns to me, brandishing her sheath as a weapon.

"I can't teach as well as Reveria and the others...So I think this is best."

Suddenly, her aura is different.

She holds her sheath in one hand, taking a defensive stance. However, her sheath and her sword have almost the same reach, so I can't let my guard down for a second.

Goose bumps shoot out of my skin a moment before my muscles react.

I draw my dagger from its sheath tucked into the back of my armor and brace myself, all in one fluid motion.

"Yes...That's good."

"...?!"

"As you did just now, I want you to perceive as much as you can from what's about to happen."

I'll have to learn from firsthand experience through sparing, as we fight. That's what she's saying.

She's telling me to learn from the impact of blade hitting blade, from reading each other's movements.

"B-but...I'm using a real blade, and you're..."

"It's fine."

Her rejection of my kindness is so swift and curt that I have to clear my throat.

Showing sympathy to an under-armed opponent is a good way to get killed. The seriousness in her eyes is screaming that at me right now.

She's overwhelming me with only a sharp glare and a blunt piece of wood.

"..."

"..."

The air between us is heating up; I could have sworn sparks were flying. The night sky is still a dull black; the sun has yet to peek over the horizon.

Aiz doesn't even twitch. Neither do I.

Although in my case, I couldn't move even if I tried.

Visions of her advance assault me. It's a near-certainty that once she takes the first step, I'll meet a strike that far exceeds my own speed and attack range.

The dagger in my sweaty palms has never felt so utterly useless.

"...You're afraid."

"?!"

"I think it's important for a solo adventurer to be afraid. But there is something else that you are afraid of."

That's the one thing I didn't want to hear, from the exact person I didn't want to hear it from.

With the same look of seriousness on her face, Aiz takes a step forward.

"I don't know what you are so afraid of...but at this rate, when you face it, you'll only be able to run away."

She's right. Those words cut deep.

Damn it...My insides are burning up. Am I shy? Or indignant? I hope it's the former.

I'm not sure why, but I feel like she hit the nail right on the head. The ultimate indicator. For a split second, the roar of a certain bovine coming up behind me shoots through my mind.

While I know it's not real, a twinge of fear floods through me.

What's this? Now my teeth are shaking? I have to get it together, fast.

Gripping the dagger in my hands as hard as I can, I take a step toward the eyes that bore holes through my soul.

There's no time to think, so I just put all my strength into my muscles and go! One more step, one more step—I'm taking the offensive.

"YAAAAAAA!!?!"

"That won't work."

—My feet leave the ground.

The sound of rending air reaches my ears. Next thing I know, I'm on my side, reeling in pain. The rock floor feels hot, my body flattened atop it.

My ribs...hurt like hell.

"Ah...Ngh?!"

"You must never become reckless. That's something you should never do, especially in the Dungeon."

I can tell she's trying to politely explain, but her words aren't reaching me.

I'd been mowed down.

I had my dagger too far out in front of me, and she hit my undefended side with her empty sheath so quickly I couldn't even see it.

Well, I saw a bit of a blur. At least I think it was a blur...

I knew. I should've known.

I knew, but...

She is just so...*fast*.

"Can you stand?"

"......!"

The question is aimed at me from above, and I peel myself slowly but surely off the floor and get back up onto my feet.

I can't breathe. My side hurts too much. I want to cry so bad, but no. I will not cry here, not now.

I clamp my front teeth down on my lip and turn to face her again.

"You aren't used to feeling pain..."

"Hnggh—?!"

"But you must not be afraid of it."

Another strike.

A frontal blow to my midsection at tremendous speed. I can see where the hit happened, but I can see my feet too...I'm flying backward again, aren't I?

Wham! The back of my head hits the stone floor. No air is going into or coming out of my lungs.

"Can you stand?" There's no pity in her voice. Somehow I manage to roll my body to the side and get up without choking.

"Being solo in the Dungeon means you can't leave any opening, ever. Keep your eyes open and sharp."

"!"

"Better."

"Hnff?!"

I thought I'd dodged that one, but she changed course.

This time she takes my knee out from under me. Next thing I know, I'm practically kissing the floor, my face burning red.

By the way, I've been wearing my light armor this entire time. And still, this pain—!

"Can you stand?" Those cold words again. I can feel blood trickling out of my nose as I once again climb to my feet.

"Just try to follow my attacks for now. Learn to read your opponent."

"Tch—?!"

"Like that."

"Buh?!"

An upward swing, and then another side sweep.

But my dagger is always a step behind. Well, it gets to the right place, but her sheath just speeds on by, on its way to nail me again. Pretty sure I spun around in midair at least once that time.

"Can you stand?" Her magic words. I'm up again.

"...You're not good at blocking, are you?"

"—?!"

Hit hit hit.

An absolute flurry of I don't know how many flashes. There's no way out! I can feel small explosions erupting all over my body as her sheath connects over and over again.

Slam! I fall to my knees, the impact echoing around me as the dust clears.

I can't stand. It's a miracle I didn't face-plant on the stone floor again.

I can hear my ragged breathing again, weak and pathetic...

"We top-class adventurers often say that many adventurers are pulled around by their own status."

"Eh......"

"Everyone depends too much on their blessing. Ability and technique are different things."

She's looking down on me. It sounds like a lecture. It's painful, but I force my eyes open and look back up at her.

She speaks slowly, as she's trying to give me information she'd learned herself.

"Technique and strategy. You lack both."

"...!"

"These things will stay with you, even if you lose your status. Such things...are all I can teach you."

She breaks eye contact with me for a moment, before looking back at me even more intensely than before.

"You have difficulty defending, so we'll focus on that. The goal of this training is for you to read my attacks, and defend. This way might be painful for you, but it will stay with you, I think. And I think...you will get closer to your goal."

She says all of this at once, looking straight into my shocked eyes.

Her golden eyes shine with sincerity as they peer into mine.

I try to make some kind of response—or any kind of sound—but nothing comes out. Aiz takes a step back and stands there, as if she's waiting for me to get up.

"Can you still stand?"

"...Thank you!"

She stared directly at my weakness, and accepted me. I have to say something.

This time spent training with her may be short, but I can't waste a second of it.

Using every fiber of my being, I force my kneeling body back up onto my feet.

I continue taking blow after blow from her sheath until the sun finally pokes its head out from the far-off eastern skyline.

Up, down, left, right—any direction he looked, his vision was filled by rugged dungeon walls covered in all sizes of rocks.

Despite the extremely high ceiling, the walls always looked like they were closing in. Boulders jutting out of the walls could fall at any moment, their overwhelming presence looming in every direction. Sources of light were scarce and unreliable, making every shadow ominous.

Of course, the footing wasn't smooth, either. The path here was an uneven gravel trail that made simply walking forward a challenge.

A cave, a mine, a deep shaft.

Many words came to mind while traveling through this level of solid rock with no pattern in its layout whatsoever.

"A long time has passed since I prowled this floor..."

The seventeenth floor of the Dungeon.

Ottar, an animal person of unusual size, continued his solitary quest on the floor, a floor typically used by Level Two adventurers.

Passing under one of the lantern-like luminescent rocks, the man's impressive frame emerged from the shadows.

He wore only light armor for protection. Despite being able to wear full-body plating, he chose to wear only enough armor to protect his vital points.

On the other hand, each piece of armor he did have was incredibly thick. It looked almost as though he had shields built into his body. Whether or not his equipment could be categorized as "light" armor, even he didn't know.

He carried an extremely large and durable bag over his shoulder. It was stuffed to its absolute limit, on the verge of bursting.

Then again, I'm not sure how long it's been since I was in the Dungeon at all.

Ottar's powerful steps made his body shake as he walked. However, where there should have been a small tremor or two in his wake, the man's feet didn't make a sound. An ominous, silencing aura followed his every movement.

His was a presence that could not be ignored, could never go unnoticed.

No monsters appeared before him, almost as if they were getting out of his way in fear.

...Jealous, huh?

His eyes and ears might have been busy scanning every nook and cranny of his surroundings, but Ottar's mind was on his recent conversation with Freya.

She'd asked him if he felt jealous.

He'd responded with complete honesty at the time. No matter what happened, he would never doubt Freya's love for him, and would continue to serve and worship her.

The Goddess Freya's love was like a wind embracing the world.

Even if someone reached out to catch it, they would fail. Her love would envelop them like a soft breeze, but the moment they thought her love was theirs, it would slip through their fingers.

Wind could not be contained. It was no one's possession. It could not be stopped.

Above all, wind sought no companion.

Wind chose a direction on a whim and drew its own path under the sky. If it should find a traveler on an open plane, it would smile and go to embrace him. But as soon as the traveler turned to face it, the wind had already moved on.

At the same time, the wind was fair.

It brought the good fortune of a cooling breeze to everyone it passed.

Sometimes, it was harsh; other times, gentle. It could flow down from the north, or waft up from the south.

It would always whisper in your ears as it blew by. Wind never stopped. Wind was eternal.

As long as Ottar and the other children were on this earth, no matter where they went, the wind would always reach them.

The fact that I'm here now, is that the answer?

What if the wind had a sky to go home to? A sky that the wind yearned for?

As a person of this world, all he could do was look up at that sky.

If looking up at it from far below triggered a petty emotion from within, then yes, it very well could be envy.

Envy and jealousy were sides of the same coin.

Childish...

A painful smile broke through his hard, emotionless exterior. This would have been very surprising, if anyone had been there to see it.

In truth, he had accepted this the moment he agreed to follow Freya's command. The wind had blown past him.

Keh! A single laugh filled with self-mockery echoed through the cave.

"...Hmm."

Ottar stopped walking.

The two boar ears sticking out of his black, thin, almost frame-like helmet twitched in response to something up ahead.

His feet changed direction to the source of the sound. Sure enough, not far from the tip of his boots, the red-black head of a bull emerged from a hole in the wall that had been hidden between two boulders.

"Mmroooo…!"

"There you are."

The bloodshot eyes of the beast found their new prey: Ottar.

Minotaur. A large-category monster with the body of a muscular man and the head of a bull. This one stood even with Ottar—perhaps even slightly taller. Starting with their height, the two combatants had a lot in common.

This was the reason Ottar had been prowling a level of the Dungeon filled with monsters far below his own level.

He was here to catch one of these violent beasts.

"Mmmmmrrrrrgh…!"

The Minotaur was getting excited.

A landform was in its grasp. This natural weapon found within the Dungeon itself was shaped like a stone ax.

The edge of the weapon was covered in a crimson liquid. Either it had just finished off an adventurer, or it had covered the ax with its own blood. Ottar couldn't see any damage on the beast itself.

This is the one, Ottar thought as his rusty eyes narrowed.

Reaching for his belt, Ottar let the bag over his shoulder fall to the floor with a loud *thud*. Along with the sound of the ground cracking on impact, metallic jangling sounds also echoed.

The sound of the crash was as good as a starting whistle for the Minotaur. It squinted its eyes as it charged headlong at Ottar.

"*Mrroooooooooah!!*"

The beast's strides hit the ground with such force that fragments of broken rocks flew backward in its wake. The Minotaur held the ax high over its head with one hand as it closed the distance.

Faced with a charging Minotaur roaring loud enough to make the walls shake, Ottar didn't bat an eye.

Holding his pack upright with his right hand, Ottar let his left arm hang loosely. He waited, unarmed, for the imminent arrival of the Minotaur.

The instant that the Minotaur planted its foot—hard enough to leave a small crater—in front of Ottar to strike, the massive man calmly raised his left arm.

"Mrooooh…Mroa?!"

"…Well done. You've been chosen."

Ottar blocked the stone ax completely.

In fact, it was the ax that took damage. The blade cracked, bits and pieces falling to the floor.

The Minotaur had put all of its weight into that attack, only to be blocked by Ottar's armor-lined arm.

While the armor itself had to be considered, this level of Defense was otherworldly. Ottar stood flat-footed on impact, but his massive body didn't budge. Without taking a defensive stance, he had taken the Minotaur's attack head-on.

Ottar looked like he was a gigantic tree, rooted to the spot, as he delivered his appraisal of the Minotaur.

It might have been instinct, but the Minotaur took one, then two steps backward, its eyes shaking in fear.

It had learned a little too late that the creature in front of it was even more of a monster than it was.

"Groh…?!"

"You are welcome to try again. If not…"

Ottar's penetrating gaze made the Minotaur freeze in terror.

Ottar watched as the stone ax fell from the Minotaur's limp fingers, and got an idea.

He reached behind his waist. Keeping his eyes locked on the Minotaur, Ottar grabbed one of the twin swords strapped to his belt—a greatsword, really—pulled it out, and tossed it in the Minotaur's direction.

"…Uwwa?"

"You demonstrated good technique. Now use this."

With an eerie charm that would've unnerved anybody watching, the Minotaur cocked its head in confusion at the hilt that was thrust at it.

Its eyes jumped nervously between Ottar and the sword over and over again, before it timidly reached out and took hold of the hilt.

The Minotaur's fingers carefully wrapped around the handle, and then it took a firm grasp.

On my life, Mistress Freya, I will not hold back.

Freya had said it herself: She'd left the boy Bell's growth in Ottar's hands.

As he had replied in that conversation, there was only one way for him to grow. Freya gave him the order, knowing full well what could happen.

This Minotaur would fight Bell.

The path Ottar was preparing for Bell was a cruel one, full of thorns.

…These might be more than mere preparations.

Up until this point, Ottar had encountered many Minotaurs, but felt them unworthy.

And all to remove the last chain within the boy's soul. To bring out the "glow" that Freya desired.

For Level One adventurers, defeating a Level Two monster like the Minotaur was next to impossible. Due to the difference in pure strength and ability, a Level One adventurer would have to have a death wish to even challenge one of them. Despite this, Ottar had given his chosen Minotaur a weapon.

Ottar's "guidance" was so severe, it bordered on tyranny.

Ottar had to admit a faintly absurd emotion had taken root in his heart. He had been forced to think about a boy named Bell.

Was he, perhaps, trying to erase the boy from Freya's sight?

Ottar asked himself that question, and answered with a resounding *no.*

Should the boy die, there was no doubt that Freya would pursue his soul. She would be willing to go all the way to the heavens to hold him in her embrace. If she weren't, she would never allow Ottar to put him into such a dangerous situation.

At this point, it didn't matter if Bell lived or died. No matter what happened, the goddess of love would be waiting for him.

This was not jealousy.

This was a *trial.*

If you're worthy of her love, survive this.

Ottar wanted proof that Bell was deserving of special treatment. Proof that he was right for Freya.

He didn't care if he lost her affection. He was willing to accept that all of her love would go to Bell alone.

However, he refused to allow someone unworthy of her attention to dirty the name of the goddess he worshiped.

Now that you have her attention, it is your duty to prove yourself worthy. It was this emotion that drove Ottar.

"Mroooaaaah!"

"…Correction. I'll have you use the weapon correctly."

Ottar easily deflected the Minotaur's first errant swing of the greatsword.

In order to prepare the beast in front of him for its role, Ottar was prepared to "train" it and fully intended to do so.

The sound of swords clashing echoed, flashes of sparks from steel colliding with steel erupted for hour upon hour.

All for Freya.

Ottar simply followed orders to the best of his ability.

"Mr. Bell, why are you a mess *before* going into the Dungeon?"

"Ha-ha-ha…Well, you know, this and that."

I weakly laugh off Lilly's question to reassure her.

Somehow I've made it through two days of Aiz's pulverization… I suppose I can call it "intense training."

Lilly gives me a look like she knows I'm hiding something, and I can't blame her. The way my body looks now, she probably thinks I was run over by stampeding monsters or something.

But I can't tell her the truth. I don't want to tell her. I don't want her to know just how unbelievably uncoordinated I am.

I couldn't block a single strike. Not one. And now I'm an absolute wreck.

I knew going into these training sessions that it would be foolish to think I'd get better right away...But to come away every time no better than a breathing punching/kicking bag, what confidence I had is gone.

I knew I wasn't that strong, but I didn't realize just how far I have to go.

There's her level, and then there's my level. There's still enough distance between us to make my head spin just thinking about it.

I walk into the lobby of Babel Tower alongside Lilly, feeling slightly depressed.

The lobby is absolutely massive. The floor is covered in large circular patterns of deep blue and white. But the most beautiful feature of the lobby has to be the stained-glass windows made to look like flowers that line the walls.

Many adventurers are here now, either on their way into the Dungeon or coming out of it. By the looks of it, most of them are, like us, about to head down into the labyrinth. However, there are some who look like they've been in the Dungeon overnight.

The contrast of the smiling, happy battle parties and the slouching, downtrodden battle parties is very striking.

The amount of loot adventurers bring back from the Dungeon tells all. Nodding slowly to myself as Lilly and I make our way through the crowd, I promise myself that we won't look like the depressed ones at the end of today.

It's a problem we all share, and nothing to scoff at. Nothing at all.

"Lilly's sorry, Mr. Bell, for making you carry Lilly's things when you're so tired."

"Don't be, it's my fault I'm tired...and anyway, I can still carry an empty backpack."

Lilly looks back at me with a very apologetic expression as we descend the first stairwell leading to the Dungeon entrance, her shoulders sinking. I crack a big smile and jump up and down a few times, saying, "See? So light!"

We've switched places—or at least that's how we're dressed right now. Basically, I'm carrying Lilly's bag, so I look like a supporter.

Meanwhile, Lilly's not wearing her usual cream-colored robe, but a sturdy-looking leather jacket on top of lightweight clothing. The icing on the cake is that she's wearing my protector like a sheath across her back, the baselard sticking out of it...so she looks to everyone else like an honest-to-goodness adventurer.

Why are we putting on this façade? To keep Lilly's existence a secret from *Soma Familia*.

Of course, Lilly is using her magic to disguise herself, but at her height and carrying something as distinct as that oversized backpack of hers, anyone with a good brain in their head might be able to connect the dots.

Prums, being one of the shorter races of people, don't usually carry bags almost twice their own size. The same goes for children of other races.

We're being extra careful, and that's why we came up with this act.

"And we'll switch out soon anyway, no need to worry about me."

Since we're just posing as each other's role, we need to be out of sight before we change back. The best spot seems to be right before the tenth level, somewhere on the ninth floor. The fog on the tenth floor is another bonus; we don't have to worry about other parties of adventurers catching a glimpse of us by accident.

We divide up the loot evenly for the return trip so that things don't look that strange when we get back to the top.

Only a few days have passed since Lilly's "death," so I think going a little overboard to protect Lilly's identity is just about right.

"Mmm...Lilly is in debt to Mr. Bell, and so recent, too. Lilly feels bad doing this to Mr. Bell..."

The tone of Lilly's voice falls, almost to the point of pouting as she spoke. The wolf ears on top of her head fold down, tips below the base.

I laugh helplessly and take another look at her.

For me, the baselard is a short sword, but it suddenly looks a lot bigger strapped to Lilly's back. That realization makes me smile. The hilt of the baselard is sticking out from under long, ash-colored hair. With eyes like golden harvest moons, she must have decided to try to be a lycanthrope today, a werewolf.

The long hair was such a change to her usual image that I didn't recognize her at first. Kind of like going from an energetic, prankster type of child to a mature, book-loving, almost royal appearance.

A few other things here and there are different, too; she's completely different from the Lilly I'm used to.

"Ah, um…what, is it a bit too much?"

She must have noticed my eyes. She's looking up at me, a bit unsure of herself as her voice quietly shakes.

I don't know if she's talking about her adventurer outfit or the werewolf transformation, but I just smile and shake my head.

I tell her that she doesn't look strange at all.

"You just look so different…a fresh look, maybe? Actually, I think you look pretty cute."

"R-really?"

"Yeah, you look good like this."

She nervously looks up at me before her eyes start to twinkle with happiness.

Lilly turns back to face forward, but her wolf ears perk up and I can see a tail swishing back and forth under her skirt.

I don't think I meant to, but seeing how Lilly responded to my compliment, seeing how happy she is, makes the corners of my mouth curve up without my even thinking.

I feel like I've got a cute little sister. And that feels…nice.

I'm watching all the adventurers who pass by us…Maybe we look like brother and sister to them.

"A hare and a wolf…"

"Wolf and bunny…"

"The rabbit is the supporter…Oh, I wonder if he'll get eaten."

"Emergency food supply in a last-resort scenario…how miserable!"

"Scary, scary. Can't judge adventurers just on looks and status, now can ya? Better keep my guard up."

…This is weird.

Why do I feel like I'm being insulted?

Whisper-whisper. I can hear all of you, right here, you know?

I've never felt this kind of kind gaze from adventurers—it's like I'm the center of attention in a pity party.

Especially the remark of that male elf a second ago. What did he mean by "how miserable"?

At least my smile is carrying me through this, but a new question jumps into my head as I take another look at "adventurer" Lilly.

I open my mouth to ask her. I can tell she's still in a really good mood just by looking at the side of her face.

"Hey, Lilly. You can't upgrade your status anymore, can you?"

"What's Mr. Bell talking about?"

"...You know, since you can't go to *Soma Familia*, you can't meet up with your god, right?"

Careful not to be overheard; I lean close to her ears as I speak.

It's impossible for Lilly to go anywhere near Soma for the time being. Therefore, the status on her back won't change.

As an adventurer, not being able to update my status would be a death sentence. I imagine it's the same for supporters, too. As I go to deeper floors, the monsters get stronger, which means it's more dangerous...

"Aren't you worried?" I ask her with concern in my eyes.

"To tell the truth, Lilly is a little worried...but it's probably fine. At the very least, Lilly's okay for now."

"R-really?"

"Yes, Lilly is good at finding ways to deal with monsters...After all, Lilly hasn't had a status update in almost half a year now and been okay."

"H-half a year?!"

Her words throw me for a loop.

I don't think I need to spell it out, but without a status update, she won't get stronger after everything she's been through. All the times she's taken a hit, fought a monster—it's all been meaningless. Talk about high risk, no reward.

Lilly grimaces when she sees the shock on my face and explains.

"To get a status update in *Soma Familia*, Lilly had to make quota."

"Wha...isn't that...?"

"Yes, it's Soma's...condition."

According to Lilly, Soma doesn't do many status updates for anyone at first.

It seems strange to me, but it sounds like he only does status updates on an "as-needed" basis. He commits all of his time and money to his one true passion, making wine. So if someone like Lilly isn't making money for him, it's a waste of his time to make her stronger. Without money from his adventurers, he can't make wine.

On top of that, his *Familia* is quite large. To update all of their statuses probably takes a very long time and would have been a real pain...

So with all that in mind, he apparently announced, "Once you meet your quota, I'll have a look at your status."

"So Lilly, you couldn't update your status without making a certain amount of money?"

"Not quite, Mr. Bell. Lilly didn't want to stand out."

"Stand out?"

"Meeting the quota regularly means that that person has skills. Lilly can't fight, and everyone knew that. So if they saw Lilly making her quota, they would get suspicious."

"Ah..." The sound escapes me before I can stop it. That's what she was getting at.

So in that case, Lilly...

"Actually, Lilly made enough to pay the quota every time, but Lilly never turned it in. If Lilly carried money, that would give her away. Not being able to update Lilly's status was a sacrifice Lilly made to hide what she was doing."

Even going to those member meetings was just to keep up appearances.

She says that she updated her status a few time after she learned her magic, but not even once over the past six months.

Not updating your status out of concern for what others in your *Familia* will think...? That *Familia* is broken.

I'd known that she was alone over there, but hearing this lets me know just how alone.

With such a meager status, she must have been able to survive day after day in the Dungeon only because she'd grown up in such a cruel environment.

She's made it this long because of her intelligence and strategies. The confidence to go into the Dungeon armed with only those, knowing your status would never improve, had to be the result of that strange upbringing.

I feel my face tighten into a frown.

"Do you despise her after all?"

"Eh?"

"The Lilly who fooled everyone and anyone. Lilly's a monster in disguise..."

Almost as if she can foresee where the conversation is going, Lilly changes the subject.

Her golden eyes don't even glance at me. She just keeps looking straight ahead.

Her voice is so soft. I can't say anything back.

"Lilly hates adventurers. With the exception of Mr. Bell, Lilly still carries a grudge...an intense loathing of them."

"......"

"No matter what Mr. Bell thinks of it, Lilly has no intension of apologizing for anything she's done...and has no remorse, either."

That's a lie.

Something inside me knows that she isn't telling the truth, but alas, I can't say it.

I can see the stern expression on her face as she voices her harsh emotions. Without much of a pause, she starts right back up again.

"Would Mr. Bell despise this Lilly after all?" she asks one more time, not breaking stride.

Her voice is normal now. Her eyes look like they're facing forward… but something's…does she notice?

The wolf ears on top of her head won't sit still. They're twitching, almost out of fear.

Blinking rapidly, I let words build up in my mind before releasing them.

I know it's not the time for a smile, but it just kind of comes out of me as I speak.

"…It's hard for me to despise people who can't be honest with themselves, I think."

"Eh?"

Her feet stop, and her head whips to face me.

"It's okay, Lilly. I like who you are, so I can't despise you, let alone hate you."

It's just how I feel.

To help her wipe away any concerns or misgivings she might have, I give her the honest truth.

I didn't know Lilly's gaze could be this strong! It feels like she's looking clear through me as her face turns red. The wolf ears that were folded down and shaking suddenly perk up.

I'm startled. Lilly's tail is going crazy under her skirt.

I may look calm on the outside, but inside, I'm absolutely bewildered. Lilly's eyes are still on me, her cheeks a rosy pink as she shrinks away.

"Asking Mr. Bell what he means would be…a stupid question, wouldn't it?"

"Huh?" Before I can ask for a clarification on *that*, she's already started walking again.

Just looking at her from behind, I'd say that she's in an even better mood than before.

Did I cheer her up? Before I know it I fall behind and rush to catch up.

"Mr. Bell's voice rings clear in Lilly's heart."

Her voice is always soft.

I try to ask her a few more times, but she won't tell me a thing. Vaguely sulking behind her, I run through our conversation silently in my head.

"Hyaaaaa!"

"Giiii!"

Little demon monsters—imps—fly at me, shrieking at the top of their lungs.

Their bodies are black from top to tail. A small horn sticks out of their oversized heads, their bodies small by comparison, giving them an unbalanced look. But they're capable of pulling off quick, sharp movements that I would have never thought possible just by looking at them.

Their tails whip around, following their bodies' twists and turns, the little hooks on the ends flicking back and forth.

"!"

Coming at me side by side, they look like they're hopping up and down in midair. I arm myself with the Divine Knife and the baselard as I face them down.

I sidestep toward the right-hand imp.

Now they can't attack me at the same time, and the one in front of me is in the other one's way.

This is as good as one-on-one. Brandishing all sorts of claws and teeth, the first imp comes up to my face with its right arm held high.

"Giii!"

"Much. Too. Slow!"

—This is nothing compared to the speed of *her* kicks!

It's planning to take a swipe at my face with its claws, so I swing the Divine Knife up to meet them.

The instant my eyes see the flashing purple arc of the blade, not only does the imp lose its claws, but the severed fingers of its right hand go flying.

"Ge, Gii?!"

Amid the imp's sharp screams of pain and surprise, I keep my momentum going by sending my body into a full spin.

I've seen so many flashes of blond hair that the form has been pounded into my mind. It's about time I tried doing her move myself.

Spinning over my right leg, I slam a powerful spinning jump kick into the monster in front of me in one swift motion.

"Higya?!"

"?!"

My left foot hits the light monster square in the chest and violently sends it flying backward.

And straight into the other imp just behind it. That imp manages to make an aerial recovery after its fingerless friend smashes into it, but I'm already going into my next attack.

Tucking my right arm behind my back, I thrust the baselard straight forward!

"Gigi?!"

My strike impales both of them.

Both bodies convulse in their death throes.

Silver liquid and guts drip out of their wounds, and their bodies' spasms make the hilt of my blade shake.

"Mr. Bell! Behind you!"

—I know!

Lilly doesn't have to warn me. I can feel the presence of another monster coming at me.

Widen your vision. Don't leave any openings.

I let go of the baselard as I spin to greet the newcomer, readying my knife in the processes.

Going on the offensive, I jump at the new imp, slashing with both blades once.

"Gee—!"

"Whoa…Nice one, Mr. Bell."

Legs. Body. Head.

I jump through the monster; all three parts of its body hit the ground as I land a meder beyond.

I'm already scanning the area, looking for more. There are still many black shadows in the fog. Their numbers haven't gone down much.

Lilly picks up the baselard for me, and I jump straight at the shadows in the mist.

We're on the tenth floor.

The floor on this level is covered with grass, and its rooms and hallways are wider than any level I've seen so far. I can't tell where it's coming from, but a thick, white fog fills the air everywhere I look.

Choosing a particularly spacious dead-end room as our base, Lilly and I are working this floor of the Dungeon today.

This is my opportunity to use what Aiz has taught me over the past two days in battle against real monsters.

After getting through that life-or-death situation, it's my duty to use what I learned from her and try harder.

"HYAAAAAAA!!"

Lilly and I are currently fighting against a swarm of imps. These little monsters are far more common than orcs down here.

They use sheer numbers as a weapon—I feel like I'm getting nowhere against them, no matter how many I take down.

Imps are clever. They might look like goblins, but there is one big difference between the two: these little bastards are smart. They know how to use a strategy.

They never attack a target one at a time; they swarm in packs. As a group, they are a serious threat. Unlike other groups of monsters I've fought before, these things have a plan. It's actually kind of impressive.

And on a floor where a big white cloud gives them constant cover, it's said that a pack of imps is more feared than even the gigantic orcs that wander around.

"Gii!"

"Hnh!"

I definitely agree. They're so fast that if I block an attack with my protector, they're already retreating back into the fog by the time I launch a counterattack. It's enough to make my mouth twitch in frustration.

Then they use the fog to sneak up on me from any and all directions. That's how I know imps are clever. They spread out and work as a team.

If I move somewhere that they can't surround me, they start clicking their tongues and shrieking at me from behind the cloud. There are eight of them, for now. More and more are coming.

A battle party of adventurers wouldn't have much trouble, but as a solo adventurer, these guys are tough to take on.

"Hyahii!"

"Hiii…"

"……"

The moment I set my feet, they spread out like a net around me.

I can see their shoulders shaking as they all laugh at me from beyond the fog.

The ring of imps is drawing closer and closer. Landing on the ground, they make their way through the grass, licking their lips like mad wolves on the hunt. I can hear everything.

If I had faced this last week, I probably would have panicked.

I might have accepted the fact I'd take a hit or two and tried to force my way out of their net.

However—

"Mr. Bell being looked at like food makes Lilly a little…annoyed!"

I'm not alone now.

Her voice comes from outside the imp ring.

An arrow suddenly slices the air from behind their backs.

"Gyya?!"

"—?!"

Lilly's arrow hit one of the imps in the back of the head. The sneak attack sends a wave of surprise through the remaining monsters.

Monsters aren't the only ones who can use the fog as cover. Lilly had hidden herself temporarily and gone undetected by the imps.

They're clever, but there is a limit to their intelligence. On the other hand, Lilly and I already had a plan for this, as well as experience in working together. We're the stronger party.

So this is what teamwork feels like. It feels good.

My turn!

Now's my chance. They're still trying to find where the arrow came from.

I slice an imp that was gawking at the golden arrow that split its comrade's head in half.

But I don't stop there. The monsters are all on the ground—easy targets for a flurry of kicks in all the confusion. Now is not the time for mercy.

"SHYAA!"

"—! Lilly!"

I catch a glimpse of them just as I finish off the imp that took her arrow.

Two of the remaining imps break away from the group and make straight for Lilly.

I may have been yelling out to her, but she doesn't flinch. A smirk on her lips, she calmly reaches inside a fold of fabric in her top and pulls out a small pouch.

"Thanks for your hard work."

Flick! Lilly flips open the pouch and releases a small cloud of powder. The imps fly right into it and immediately start hacking and coughing.

Koff! Koff! The sudden purple dust cloud permeates through their bodies, the imps coughing so hard that they fall out of the air.

Purple Moth Scales. A drop item.

Lilly just used a poison grenade made from these scales.

It's fast-acting, unlike the purple moth's scales by themselves, and is strong enough to poison smaller monsters on contact.

—Clever girl! Looks like she wasn't lying about being able to handle monsters!

Lilly taking a quick step back is my cue to spring into action.

I make eye contact and give her a little nod, to let her know I'll take it from here.

I can't help but smile a little.

"All right!"

I take a deep breath and hold it as I jump into the cloud of purple dust. Then, *slash*.

Using both of the shorter blades, one in each hand, I slay both imps without taking a breath.

The only ones left now are...

"...Mr. Bell, something a little bigger is here!"

"!"

A small tremor shakes the room. I know what it is immediately.

An orc. I've had dealings with this type of pig-headed monster before. Standing close to three meders tall, the beast is coming toward us bare-handed.

Of course there are still a few imps around, but they look like minions waiting for the boss's command as I get a better feel for the surroundings.

There's a bad bat above me. It's a black bat–type monster with sharp claws and a really distracting scream. It's enough to make me feel dizzy in combat.

The remaining imps on the ground take to the air, their tails between their legs, and join their allies behind the fog.

"So many..."

"Yes, it's very rare that this many types of monsters gather like this. What should Lilly do? Lead the orc away?"

Lilly set her backpack down on the grass and loaded an arrow into her crossbow as she made her suggestion.

I squint my eyes as I think it through.

With the fog in the way, I can't tell exactly how many of each monster there is. Except for the orc, anyway. I don't feel comfortable telling Lilly to leave my side when I don't know what we're up against...

I return both of my knives to their sheaths, and shake my right wrist.

"Mr. Bell?"

"Heh-heh. I might be relying on this a bit too much..."

I smile and nod to let her know what's coming. I think she gets the message because she quickly scrambles out of the way.

Now I have a clear shot.

With the various cries and shrieks of the monsters ringing in my ears, I raise my right arm and take aim.

"FIREBOLT!"

Bolts of scarlet flame carve their way through the sea of fog, wiping out everything in their path.

"Can I ask you something, Lilly? Do you think I'm depending on my Magic too much?"

Holding a sandwich in my hand, I ask Lilly for her opinion.

After clearing out most of the monsters, we decided to take a rest. So we've come back to the first room on the tenth level. The stairs connecting to the ninth are behind me.

This is the only room on the lower tenth that doesn't have any fog. Since the chances of a sneak attack are much higher everywhere else, I think it's safe to say that this is the least dangerous room on this level.

I'm eating the usual lunch from Syr as I wait for Lilly's answer.

Now that I think about it, Syr's handmade sandwiches are always a little strange. The more I chew, the more new and exciting varieties of bitterness come to the surface.

She tried something new again today, but it tastes like a swamp... It's rude of me to think that, so I better keep chewing to make up for it. But honestly, I'm on the verge of tears.

My lunches are getting scarier and scarier every day.

"Hmmm...Lilly doesn't think it's a problem...Mr. Bell's Magic is very easy to use, too..."

Lilly tilts her head from side to side, as if sloshing the ideas around in her head, while holding a modest-sized piece of bread in her hands.

Her lips wrap around the bread whenever she takes a bite; it's very cute. Taking her last bite, she wipes her mouth with a napkin before continuing.

"Because it's easy to use, it might be easy to get in a habit of casting it. But rather than depending on it, Lilly thinks it's become one of Mr. Bell's basic maneuvers."

"Well, when you put it like that…"

It lined up pretty well, actually.

Firebolt is Swift-Strike Magic.

Each Magic has a spell you have to chant to activate it…so basically, there's nothing you have to save up.

For me, Magic is like a punch or a kick that I don't use as often. Maybe it's just another technique for me to use in combat.

"Lilly thinks about it like this. Mr. Bell's Magic is very effective, but its role is much more limited than other Magic."

"Um…and that would be…?"

"As a finishing move."

The moment she said that, I immediately think of the picture of a certain hero on page one of a *Tales of Adventure* book.

A young elfish warrior summoning a blizzard to face down a fearsome beast.

"Magic is the ace up the sleeve. You could even call it a last resort, because if it's powerful enough, Magic can take down an enemy at a level higher than the caster. Mr. Bell's Magic is very easy to use, but it might be limited to a role as the killing blow."

Sure, I can use it like nobody's business, but that doesn't mean it's all that powerful.

Blow for blow, it's nothing like the kind of Magic Lilly's talking about.

I make a timid face as I listen to the rest of Lilly's explanation.

"Since the Magics with long trigger spells are more powerful, they have the ability to bring the caster back from the edge of defeat. They're a way to perform miracles."

So if you turn that around…

"My Magic is too weak to do that…?"

"No, no. That's not what Lilly's saying. It's the idea of quality over quantity, or quantity over quality. Mr. Bell's Magic is formidable… At least for Lilly, a magic that can be cast suddenly is much scarier than one that is more powerful but takes time. Mr. Bell's 'Firebolt' is scary because it can't be avoided."

Lilly smiles as she finished.

I guess she's trying to say that my Magic is plenty intimidating as it is now.

It's just that the impact of each strike lacks the power of other Magics.

So if I were to face a particularly strong monster—something with very high Defense—then my Magic won't be as effective as other offensive magic would be.

Well, yeah, Magic isn't perfect. I know that anyone can find a downside to any Magic in the book…

I don't know if it's because I've fantasized about Magic since I was a kid, but realizing the weakness in my own…I feel, I don't know, sad somehow.

Lilly must have read the disappointment on my face because when I look up at her, she's all smiles.

"Mr. Bell, oh Mr. Bell? Lilly thinks Mr. Bell's Magic is one of the better ones, okay? No spell, lightning speed, but it's growing very fast, too. That Magic is ahead of the pack."

"……?"

"It's very difficult to use Magic that requires time to cast. Does Mr. Bell think that monsters will wait for someone to finish the incantation? And since those Magics can't be used very often, they can't grow. Magic has to be used for it to get more powerful; the status won't change."

So if the caster doesn't have a chance to use their Magic, their Magic Skill won't improve.

In that case, with a little time and effort on my part, my Magic could become many times more powerful than it is now, if I use it frequently.

"As Magic Skill increases, so do the effects of each spell. Lilly knows this because her Magic changed as her Magic Skill went up. It has nothing to do with combat, but it could do more things."

Lilly's magic, "Cinder Ella," has a limit to how much it can change the overall shape of her body. For the most part, she can only change to look like other short races or children of taller ones. Apparently she gained the ability to copy different types of clothing as her Magic Skill went up. However, she needs an example to copy for it to work.

Turns out her clothes right now are the result of her Magic (although she said that the effect ends if she takes a hit).

I take a long, hard look at my hand.

Thinking back, the size and power of the flaming bolts *have* gotten much thicker and stronger since the day I first cast Firebolt.

"Back to the original question: If Mr. Bell is depending on his Magic too much, or not. Since Magic gets stronger the more it's used, Lilly doesn't think it can be helped. Mr. Bell's Magic could be considered a close-quarters combat technique, and he might neglect the others if he uses it too much, so it is difficult…But Lilly thinks Mr. Bell is doing okay as he is."

Lilly's very convincing, so I give her a firm nod.

It's the opinion of the one person who's spent the most time with me as an adventurer.

"Mr. Bell's Magic element may be simple, and its power average, but its potential to grow makes it great. Be confident, Mr. Bell."

I blush a little as she flashes her teeth in a big smile.

Thanks to Lilly's seal of approval, I feel a lot better about my Magic.

Actually, to tell the truth, I feel relieved.

I say a quiet "Thanks" before standing up.

"Up for some more prowling?"

"Yes. Lilly will support Mr. Bell wherever he may go."

That's a strong way to say that…All I can do is smile.

The two of us work together, giving our all against the monsters of the lower tenth after that.

CHAPTER 3

BLACK RAID

"……"

My eyes slowly open.

I can see a clear, blue sky.

Staring up at it, I can feel a light breeze on my skin. It must have come down from up there.

My whole body hurts. What was I doing…? Oh yeah—flashes of light, the sudden impacts over and over again—all of them were *her* attacks.

Did I get owned again…?

I've lost count at this point; if I could move my neck, it would be drooping.

This is my training with Aiz on the top of the city wall.

These sessions are getting more and more violent by the day, to the point where me getting knocked out is not just normal, but expected. More than likely, that's exactly what happened this time, and I'm sprawled out on the stone floor.

Just when I get around to trying to figure out how long I've been out, I notice something soft supporting my head…just happened to be there.

Two golden eyes come into my line of sight, forehead first, as I lay on my back.

"Are you okay?"

"…Waah?!"

That's Aiz's face! Suddenly wide-awake, I let out a strange grunt in surprise.

Rolling away from her, I put a little distance between us before climbing to my feet. Sure enough, when I turn around, there she is. Aiz is just calmly sitting on her feet, knees directly on the stone surface.

…My head was in her lap, again.

Ever since that incident in the Dungeon—the one where I used my Magic so much that I passed out—Aiz has put my head in her lap whenever I get knocked unconscious. I wonder if that day in the Dungeon is the reason why…

Don't get me wrong, I love the fact that she's doing this for me… But part of me wants to die. It's just so pathetic in so many ways.

Aiz looks at me with confusion and pats her knees a few times. *Tap tap tap.* It's an invitation to come back.

I shake my head no.

"Is your body feeling better?"

"…Yes."

She gestures for me to take a seat next to her. My face is always reddish when we're together, but I feel my cheeks go slightly darker as I sit down at her side.

The rock is really cold on my rear end, but I try to relax and lean back into the wall behind me.

Today turned into a full training day with Aiz.

As for why—I got a message from Lilly that she had to help out at the shop she's living at today, so she couldn't go into the Dungeon with me.

So rather than go into the Dungeon by myself, I told Aiz about my circumstances. I feel a little bad about training beyond our usual time, but here we are, still working under the blue sky.

It's about break time now.

"Um, a-am I getting any better, at all?"

"…Why do you ask?"

"Well, you know, I'm getting knocked out a lot recently…"

I'm getting nervous just thinking about how close my shoulders are to hers, so I start a conversation.

Aiz looks at the side of my face in silence; I don't have the guts to turn to face her.

"You are, and very quickly…Enough to surprise me."

"Eh? B-but…"

"It's most likely my fault, that you keep passing out…I forget my own strength."

"S-so that means—?!"

She then slowly closes her eyes about halfway. I've figured out that whenever she does that, she's feeling sad.

Her shoulders sink as her mood falls. I try to cheer her up, but at the same time, something feels strange.

She's the shooting star far beyond my reach.

That hasn't changed, but seeing her like this makes her seem much more human. The person beside me doesn't look like the Kenki.

I can't put it into words...This doesn't feel real.

The lofty, sublime, and ever-beautiful Aiz Wallenstein has some strange points, just like a normal girl...I only feel this way about her during our breaks.

I only started thinking about this after seeing her be depressed because she couldn't hold herself back during training.

"...Can I ask you a question?"

"Huh?"

My train of thought had taken me far away when Aiz's voice brings me back into the present.

Turning to face her directly, I find that she's hiding her sadness with a very serious expression.

"How are you getting strong so quickly?"

"S-strong...?"

Her choice of words made my eyes spin for a moment.

Strong—I didn't know someone could use that word when talking about me. This has never happened before. How am I supposed to react?

All the most pathetic experiences I've ever had flash through my head. I just want to curl up in a hole and bury myself right now. But that look in her eye makes me stop and think for a moment.

How I got strong...No, *why* I've tried to become strong up until now...

"...You see, there's a person that I want to catch up to. I put all my effort into chasing them, and now I'm like this...So..."

My brain's going a mile a minute; my words aren't coming out right.

Then again, the "person" I'm chasing is sitting right next to me, but I can't say that directly to her! Way too embarrassing.

Feeling a bit disoriented, I manage to string a few more words together.

"...I think it's because there's a goal I have to reach, no matter what."

I think I see Aiz's eyes open a bit wider when she hears me.

She sits silently for a moment before leaning her head backward.

"I see."

She wraps her arms lightly around her knees and just looks up at the sky.

A slightly stronger breeze rolls through; Aiz's blond hair tickles my nose.

"...I know the feeling."

"Huh?" The sound jumps out of my throat in response to her sudden words.

"I, too..."

A strong burst of wind blew in, and took the rest of her words with it. I have no idea what she said after that.

This wind is strong enough to make me shut my eyes.

It's a sudden cool breeze from the west. The wind sounds like a flute as it passes through the wide avenues of the city.

When I finally reopen my eyes, there she is, sitting in exactly the same position like nothing happened. Her eyes are still gazing skyward.

"E-er..."

"?"

"Ah, um, it's nothing."

She tilts her head, showing almost no emotion on her small face. I can't say anything.

What's the point in asking her? I ask myself as I sit in front of this girl, with a look in her eyes that I've never seen on her before. They've made so many expressions—but not this one. It stops my thoughts in their tracks.

Our conversation stops there. Just when I was starting to feel restless.

A bell rings from Orario's eastern bell tower. It's noon.

I let the deep echoes of the bell fill my ears. It sounds a lot like church bells, actually. But at the same time, I hear the sound of horses coming from outside the city, beyond the wall. There must be some merchants trying to enter the city gates, and the Guild is conducting an inspection of their cargo.

We're sitting on a wide stone path on the top of Orario's city wall. There's a barrier about chest-high on both sides of the path. A gorgeous view of the city spreads out on the inside of the wall. Looking the other way, I can see a large mountain range surrounded by dense forests and wide plains going far into the distance.

Listening to the unusual mix of bells and outside commotion, it hits me: the weather is spectacular today.

My eyelids droop as I feel the bright warmth of the sun and gaze at the white, puffy clouds in the distance.

"Haah…"

"……?"

I turn my head to find the source of that sound, only to see Aiz with her hand over her mouth.

Her small mouth is open, lips quivering slightly…she's yawning.

Bathed in the warmth of the sun, she puts her arm back around her knees like nothing happened.

Shortly thereafter—

"Shall we practice napping?"

"Huh?"

My eyes shrink into little dots on my face as I consider her rather strange suggestion.

Turning her head to face me, Aiz suddenly starts speaking with vigor.

"You have to be able to sleep anywhere at any time, while in the Dungeon, after all."

"……"

"It's important to recover your strength quickly."

She might have a good point.

I usually spend the day prowling the Dungeon and go home at night, but if I want to go deeper, I'll need to spend nights down there, too. That means that I'll need to be able to sleep knowing that there are monsters in there, too, and without a nice warm bed. It's a problem that I, as an adventurer, will have to face sooner or later.

Aiz explains the importance of getting to sleep quickly, regardless of location, with all seriousness.

But as for me, I can't even look at her without my face contorting into an embarrassed smile.

"Are you...maybe...sleepy?"

"......"

She then slowly turns her whole body my way and says:

"This is training."

"R-right."

Her face is just a few celches away from mine. Sweating profusely, I nod again and again until she backs away.

She looks a bit angry. Did I hit a nerve...? But her cheeks...it's only just a little, but they're turning pink.

I...I can't breathe...! What am I, an idiot...?!

"W-well um...are we going to sleep here?"

"Yes."

She gives a quick nod as she slides away from the wall, before lying down on the stone surface.

This goes without saying, but these stones are hard. To the builder's credit, the path on top of the wall is very well constructed, but there are some uneven places here and there.

But Aiz doesn't care about that. She lies right down and starts dozing. So this is the true power (?) of a top-class adventurer.

For someone who has to be able to rest anywhere in the deepest parts of the Dungeon, sleeping here—without any difficulty, I might add—might just be a walk in the park.

"Are you not going to sleep?"

"Ah, um…No, I'll sleep."

Feeling really awkward as she stares up at me, I make a little space between us before sitting down.

She's sprawled out on her side, completely defenseless. If I were to do something impure—not that I would!—I'd have the opportunity… But then I see the blade of her saber, glistening in the afternoon sunlight. That puts an end to such thoughts rather quickly. Trying to pull a fast one on her all but guarantees she'll mount my severed head on a wall somewhere.

And it's not like she isn't somewhat aware of what's going on around her. Maybe this is another way for a master to test their student? It could be her own style of a test.

…And this *is* training, after all.

"…Well, then…"

Cautiously inching my body forward, I lay down next to Aiz.

Yeah, I'm not sleepy, at all. My heart is beating too loud for me to even relax.

I take a quick glance at Aiz out of the corner of my eye. But the moment I see her closed eyes, I immediately look away.

I squeeze my eyes closed so tight that I feel wrinkles pop up all over my forehead.

Sleep, sleep, SLEEP! I command myself as I lay on my back.

"……?"

I hear it a second later: light breathing.

I risk opening an eye and turning my head, only to find Aiz with her eyes closed and out like a light.

That was…quick.

I know it's important to regain your strength in the Dungeon, but maybe she's used to sleeping in places like this?

Or maybe she was just that tired…?

"…*ve, Bell.*"

…Wha?

"Make a move, Bell."

I know that voice. What's it doing in the back of my head?

There's no way I could mistake that for something else…That's

ｚ
ｚ
ｚ...

Gramps's voice. He raised me; I'll never forget the sound of his voice. And now it's coming from inside my head, for some reason.

It's getting stronger by the moment. Am I being haunted? Or hallucinating...?

...*Hey, what's going on...?*

Aiz is getting closer...?

It has to be an illusion. I squint my eyes like I do when I get up in the morning.

There should be enough room between us that one or two more people could fit...so why is...

"Now's your chance, Bell!"

Now her face is really, really close!

?!

That's when I notice what's wrong.

We're lying face-to-face; the distance between us is gone.

Aiz is getting closer and closer to me...Wait, no! She hasn't moved a single celch this whole time!

So...so that means...!

"Go, now!"

I'm getting closer to her?!

My heart had been beating like there's no tomorrow up until now, but it almost stops on the stop. My body is suddenly drenched in a cold sweat.

It's really happening! My body, it's getting closer to Aiz!

WHY?! HOW?! Am I really about to do something like...*that*?!

She'll kill me!

"Take the opening!"

GAHHHH?!

Even closer.

Her face is getting bigger, big enough that I can see every detail of her innocent, sleeping face.

Her smooth, pure white skin. The nape of her neck...soft, delicate pink lips.

My face turns an intense red as her pristine visage comes even closer.

Wait! Wait wait wait! I scream inwardly.

Almost as if I were being controlled by Gramps's "guidance," my body starts to move into an even closer position. And skillfully enough to keep Aiz unaware of my presence. What the hell is going on?!

Am I seriously going to...to *her*...?!

"Give 'er a kiss!"

DAAAAAAAAAAHHHHHHHHHHHHHHHHHHH?!

"—No! Wait! Bell!!"

I can hear the Goddess Hestia's voice ringing in my ears, telling me just how wrong this is.

"Do you seriously think I'd let you take advantage of a defenseless, sleeping girl like this?! I don't remember raising you to be like that!"

A shiver suddenly runs down my whole body.

Now it feels like my body is being pulled by strings, like I'm a puppet. But I feel...strangely normal.

Yes, the goddess is absolutely right...!

"If you try and kiss her like this, I'll never forgive you, Bell! Got that? NEVER!"

She sounds awfully desperate, and that tone in her voice sends yet another round of cold sweat out of every pore in my body. I try to put more space between us.

My body shakes back and forth, my progress excruciatingly slow. It's like two titans of will are fighting for control, and my body is their battlefield.

The "light" of the goddess and the "darkness" of Gramps clash over and over.

"Now, get away from her—"

"The real war starts now!"

"—Agh. Hey! What do you think you're—gahh!"

—The goddess lost!

Her voice falls silent after a wave of dark energy tipped the scale the other way.

What space was left between Aiz and I quickly vanishes, our noses touching.

"......!"

She's so beautiful, sleeping peacefully with her eyes closed.

She's so close that my eyes can't focus on one spot. My mind and body are burning just looking at her.

With Gramps's hearty laugh filling my head, I rotate my neck so that my lips will touch hers.

"Wait—just—!"

"!!"

I have control over my body!

My head twitches backward, away from Aiz, as my body rolls away from her.

My heart is beating at an impossible rhythm; it feels like it's going to explode. I'm practically lying in a pool of my own sweat.

My back to Aiz, I can hear Gramps's sigh of disappointment. Slowly, very slowly, I look back over my shoulder at the girl.

"......"

She's still asleep.

Her eyes closed just like before, her breath so quiet and delicate that I have to really focus to hear it.

All the tension suddenly drains out of me.

...*wait?*

With my heart still beating against my ribs, I catch a glimpse of Aiz's lips mouthing something at me.

Not "stop"...but "wait."

That's what she's saying, I'm sure of it.

I start to think about the meaning of that word when a sudden surge of guilt flows over me. I put my hands on each side of my head in agony. Just what the hell was I about to do...?!

*AGGGGGHHHHH...*I silently scream next to her, thinking about what I was about to do in shame.

"...Haaa."

I lay there for a few more minutes, the shame and guilt radiating out of me.

I let out a long sigh before putting even more space between us.

This won't happen again. Rolling over onto my back, I stare up at the sky.

The events of the past few minutes on replay in my mind, I somehow manage to cool off my burning face.

"......"

A steady, rhythmic breathing reaches my ears. I'm not even listening for it.

Should I? Should I not? Promising myself not to repeat what just happened, I slowly turn my head to look at her, my cheek on the cold stone path.

"......"

Her face is close—just as close as I remember it from when was lying down before our "practice."

The sound of her breath reaches my ears. One lock of her blond hair has fallen over her cheek.

I've seen this somewhere in the *Tales of Adventure*...Which hero was it?

Oh yeah, the princess who was cursed to sleep for a hundred years.

She would only awaken when her hero found her, the princess trapped in eternal sleep.

The character I read about so long ago and the girl in front of me have so much in common, right down to their breathing rhythm.

"......"

I lie there, staring at her peaceful face for a moment before looking away again.

Looking up at the azure sky, I lift up my left hand, pinch my cheek and give it a little tug.

Yep, that's pain.

It feels like a dream...

Being next to her like this, spending time alone together like this.

I put my left hand back down and let myself be drawn in by the sky.

I let my emotions go, my heart feel like it has finally calmed down.

Here we are, just two people lying down on top of the city wall, bathed in warm sunlight. I let my eyelids drop and fall into a deep slumber.

The Orario City Wall was not only strong, it was massive.

It surrounded the city like a ring. An uneven stone path sat on top of the ring and went all the way around the city.

Citizens were forbidden to use it, so there was almost never anyone on the path.

The purpose of the city wall wasn't to keep things out, but to keep things in. So the inner guard wall of the path was high enough that the path couldn't be seen from even the tallest buildings. It went without saying that it couldn't be seen from the ground, either.

The chances of someone seeing the two of them together was next to nothing.

No one could spy on their training, let alone catch a glimpse of them.

It was safe to say that Aiz's plan to train Bell here, in order to avoid an issue between their *Familias*, had gone very well up to this point.

"My goodness, you're in plain sight up here."

There was however, a place from where their training *could* be seen: the highest room of the tallest tower in Orario—Babel.

Sitting in a fancy chair facing the glass wall of her own room, Freya watched their training with interest.

Even with the high guard wall, Freya's room was high enough that she could see over it, and watch to her heart's content.

"That girl's soul…the Kenki is blinding…"

Freya was on the fiftieth floor of Babel Tower, in the middle of the city. The distance between her and the humans was much too far to see, but Freya's eyes were different. She could clearly see their souls shining on top of the wall.

Her Acumen Eyes allowed her to see the quality of any person's soul by color. She had those eyes on a clear, colorless, glowing spirit and an extremely bright, golden pyre of a soul. There was no way her eyes could have missed them.

She noticed them training beyond the early morning hours, and had been watching their training session all day.

"And yet…things are getting interesting."

A small smile formed on her lips as Freya ran her fingers through her silver hair and behind her ear.

As her disciple set the stage far below in the Dungeon, the star of the show was receiving training from that female warrior, as her student.

It would be the monster trained by Ottar against the human boy trained by the Kenki.

Freya's heart was alive with excitement as she thought about this turn of events. It could turn out far more interesting than she had ever thought possible.

"……"

Her silver eyes fell on the two humans for a moment.

They were lying down, as if they'd fallen asleep. Freya watched their souls glow with a smile on her face. *Tap, tap, tap.* Her fingers restlessly hit the armrest of her chair over and over.

Then her other hand came up and started fiddling with her hair, wrapping it around her fingers. That's when she suddenly stopped moving.

She'd finally noticed what she was doing. She grimaced and lightly laughed at herself and whispered under her breath.

"Ahh, so now *I'm* jealous, of *her…*"

I can hardly believe this, she thought, as she had another laugh.

For a god such as her to feel that way about a child was absolutely absurd, and she laughed at herself for it.

It was how she felt when Hestia and the boy were together. But this time, the feeling was much stronger.

The fact that this golden pyre was shaping the clear light was a little—just a little—off-putting for her.

A small bud of jealousy was starting to bloom in her substantial chest.

"...This is irritating," she whispered under her breath. She sat up in her chair and looked out the top of her glass window into the clouds.

A few moments passed.

She closed her eyes before opening them just slightly...and filled the room with her exquisite laugh.

"I wonder, just how strong are you now?"

Settling back into her chair, Freya's eyes once again fell on the boy.

Her gaze was filled with an urge to tease him—and something a bit more vicious: jealousy.

Maybe it's time to have some more fun with him, she thought with a dark smile gracing her lips.

A sadistic grin reflected off the inside of the long glass wall of her room in Babel Tower.

Following the long corridors and steep stairwells inside Orario's City Wall, we finally arrive at the door that leads to the city and open it.

The heavy wooden door creaks as it swings to the side, to reveal a back alley cloaked in shadow.

The alleyway itself is strewn with dirty, wooden boxes, piles of old building material, and scrap metal. It looks like someone was using this spot as a storage area and forgot about it, as well as the door in the city wall. Aiz and I make our way through the bric-a-brac and into the maze of backstreets.

We continued training after waking from a surprisingly refreshing nap, before making our way down here in the late afternoon.

"A-Aiz, don't worry about it. It was an accident, anyway......"

"It's not a problem. My stomach is empty, too."

...In the middle of a flurry of swift attacks, you see, my eyes following only the shadows of her movements, my stomach decided to...speak up.

Aiz saw me blush out of embarrassment and suggested getting a light snack. That's why we're here now.

I know I only ate breakfast today, just still...ugh...

Holding back tears of shame, I follow Aiz with my shoulders down around my ribs somewhere.

The unguarded door that Aiz found to the normally restricted city wall was on the outer edge of northeastern Orario. After turning many tight corners in the alleyway, we come out into one of the wider backstreets, close enough to Main Street to hear people busily going about their business.

This spot is filled with houses and lined with fancy, pole-shaped magic-stone lamps. This is all new to me. My head on a swivel, I take in as much as I can.

"Can I ask where we're going?"

"North Main. Tiona told me about a potato puffs stand over there."

That's her answer. Tiona...must be another member of *Loki Familia.*

Right now, Aiz and I are going through the backstreets because we can avoid being seen. And while it's great that we're being so cautious, something else is making me nervous being alone with Aiz right now.

Potato puffs...I know that from somewhere. Why do I have a bad feeling about this?

My ears pick up on the hustle and bustle of Main Street. We're here.

The sun is still in the sky, but very close to setting. The sky is starting to turn red. North Main is alive with elves, dwarves, and demihumans of all races heading home after work. We really stick out, being in armor and all...Wait, it's not me. They're looking at Aiz. I try to make myself as small as possible as we make our way through the gawking crowd.

Aiz isn't paying them any attention; her eyes are scanning the buildings. She must have found what she was looking for because she suddenly turns into a side street.

It's not too wide, maybe one of those horse-drawn taxis could fit through, but that's about it. I take a few steps down the street, and there it is. A street stall selling potato puffs.

—But my body freezes as it hits me.

"Welcome to our...stand?"

A clerk greets us as Aiz pulls back the cloth "door" to reveal...the goddess. Time stands still.

The goddess's face is stuck somewhere between a welcoming smile and a look of wide-eyed shock.

Reflected in her gaze are Aiz...and me, standing right next to her. Suddenly, my face is blue.

"......"

"......"

"Two sweet-bean potato puffs, please."

Aiz happily orders potato puffs as the goddess and I stand like statues next to her.

The "clerk" slowly starts to move, putting two fresh puffs with frosting on them into a bag and saying, "That's eighty vals," as she holds out the bag. Aiz sets the money on the counter, says, "Thank you," and takes the food out of the goddess's frozen hand.

The clerk suddenly loses her composure, and all the muscles in her face twitch as she runs out from behind the counter and in front of us.

Meanwhile, I'm experiencing an avalanche of cold sweat running down my back.

"—WHAT THE HELL ARE YOU DOINGGGGGGG?!"

"S-S-S-SO-SO-SO-SORRY!"

In front of the goddess's blaze of emotion, all I can do is scream my apology at the top of my lungs.

I never told her about my training sessions with Aiz.

By and large, it's not good to have connections with someone in another *Familia*. I know that my goddess isn't on good terms with

Aiz's goddess, Loki. And then there's the fact that the goddess really doesn't like Aiz herself, either…

I knew that she wouldn't allow me to train with Aiz if I told her, so I accepted the risk that something like this might happen, and kept it a secret.

"Walking around, alone, with the Kenki?! What's gotten into you, Bell?!"

"Th-there's a reason for this, s-so…!"

"No excuses! Spill it, now! …Get away from her! GET!!"

The goddess's voice shrieks as she practically dives between Aiz and me.

Aiz looks slightly troubled as she glances down at the goddess, who was looking up at her like an enemy while creating a physical barrier.

"Explain! Why are you with the Kenki?!"

"Eh, um, you see, we just happened to bump into each other…?!"

"…NO ONE CAN LIE TO A GOD!!"

She spins to face me, throwing up her arms and screaming, "UGAAAHH!!!" I shrivel up into a little ball, tears leaking out of my eyes.

Her jet black twin ponytails seem to come alive, smacking me in the face as the goddess shakes with anger.

She's passing judgment on me for my little white lie that was supposed to comfort her!

"Um…I'm teaching him, how to fight."

Aiz, who had been silently watching this unfold, speaks for the first time.

It must have been really hard to watch. She tells the truth right away, trying to protect me.

The goddess's neck snaps around, eyes blazing as she looks back at Aiz. The moment she understands what the girl had said, the goddess's shoulders start shaking violently.

"Bell, you haven't by any chance shown her your status, have you?"

"Of course I haven't. Why would there be any reason to?"

"So that means that your growth speed hasn't been noticed...?!"

I couldn't really make out what she said there, but I can see her staring down (or up, in this case) Aiz like she was her sworn enemy.

Without warning, the goddess wraps her arms around my chest.

Wha-what's going on here?!

"You're trying to claim my Bell for your own, aren't you! I won't let that happen. I was with him first, no matter what you say!"

"G-Goddess, what are you doing?!"

"Wha...Waaaah?! B-Bell, why are you acting so bold?!"

ME?!

"Oh, Hestia darling, you're making a scene. I can't sell anything like this. If you're going to quarrel, take it out back, would you please!"

"Ah! S-sorry, Gram! You two, you're coming with me!"

An older animal person scolds the goddess from behind the counter. The goddess then glares at both Aiz and me in turn, before flicking her wrist and pointing outside the stand.

I'm spent; I feel like a shell of my usual self. But the goddess grabs my wrist and pulls my listless body out into the street. Aiz follows quietly without saying anything.

The goddess guides us behind the stand and around a few corners to a narrow backstreet. I don't think anyone has set foot back here in a while...

We stand in silence for a moment, the three of us in a loose circle.

"...Hmmm. First off, I want to know *everything* about what's been going on."

I'm so glad that she managed to cool off a bit. Gathering my thoughts, I apologize again for keeping her out of the loop and tell her everything that's happened, starting with our chance meeting at the Guild.

Every few sentences, I make sure to get an affirmative nod from Aiz before continuing.

The goddess listens to my explanation with her arms folded across her chest, before nodding her head a few times when I finish.

"...All right, I see. And it's time that the two of you call it quits."

"Wha...?!"

"Is this bad...?"

"Yes, Miss Wallensomething. Never come near my Bell again. You have your own place, right? And considering your *Familia*'s goddess, I think this is the best—mmphmphfl?!"

I'm mentally on all fours, bowing down and begging for forgiveness, as I reach out and cover the goddess's mouth with my hand.

"Please, Goddess. Just a little bit more. I beg you to let me continue training with Aiz for just a little longer."

"......?"

Aiz tilts her head as I turn the goddess away from her, and lean in close to speak with her quietly.

"A little longer, why would you ask?...!"

"Just two more days! That's all! That's all that she said she'd work with me!"

I explain that she'll leave for an "expedition" with *Loki Familia* in three days and bow my head over and over, hoping that she'll give me permission.

I tell her from the bottom of my heart that I need to learn as much as I can from Aiz in this short amount of time.

"I won't waste a second of training time! This is to help me earn more money in the dungeon! So please, Goddess...!"

"Gahh...!"

I've been asking her over and over again as if my life depended on it for a few minutes by now, bundling words and promises together like there was no tomorrow.

But the goddess just growls and glances at me before letting out a long sigh.

"You're too naïve; me, too..."

"Goddess......"

"...Really, just two more days. I'm serious here."

As soon as I hear those words, my body, mind, and soul all bow as far as they can.

Repenting for all the trouble my selfishness is causing her, I'm extremely thankful.

The goddess's only requirement is to make absolutely sure that no one else in *Loki Familia* finds out about our activities. That's enough to receive her approval for two days' worth of training with Aiz.

"I'll say this, though: The moment you do anything *else* with Bell, I will unleash Hell. Got that?"

"Yes."

"And seducing him is right out…!"

"Yes…?"

The goddess is giving Aiz a very strange warning. What's she talking about…? I can't take it—I have to step in.

"Well, then, I'll be observing the rest of your training session today."

"Huh?!"

"What's with that face, Bell? It's my duty as your goddess and guardian to make sure my precious child is okay?"

"Eh, um, w-what about your job…?"

"I'm taking the rest of the day off."

She tells us to wait a moment before returning to the potato puffs stand. I watch her go, scratching my cheek as beads of sweat roll down my face.

I look at Aiz, asking her with my eyes if this is okay. She smiles at me and nods.

"She is a nice goddess, isn't she…"

"…Indeed."

We go back up to the city wall with the goddess in tow. Aiz and I set to work immediately to make up for lost time.

I don't know if it was because I didn't want the goddess to see something embarrassing, but I don't get knocked out the rest of the day. I get beaten to a pulp, but I think I do pretty well.

By the time we reach a good stopping point, it's already night.

"Hey, Bell, look at yourself. You're a total mess. You should stop now—Aiz Wallensomething is just using you as her personal punching bag."

"G-Goddess…"

We enter the long stone corridor leading out of the city wall, the goddess taking potshots at my pride.

There are almost no windows in here, so it's extremely dark. She has a tight hold of my hand as we go down a stairwell, but I'm on the verge of tears. She seems to be in a great mood right now, though; I can see the outline of a big smile on her face.

Is it that much fun to torment me?

But then again, after what nearly happened today, I need to grin and bear this…

"We've arrived…"

Aiz is a few paces in front of us, holding a portable magic-stone lamp (she said it was a necessity for adventurers to have one) in her hand.

Surrounded by the echoes of Aiz's boots on the stone floor, we reach the bottom of the stair and out the exit door. Leaving the slightly damp air inside the wall, a rush of cool, dry air envelops my body.

A golden moon and hundreds of twinkling stars fill the dark night sky.

"Um, Goddess? We made it outside, you don't have to hold my hand anymore…"

"What are you talking about, Bell? This road isn't bright like Main Street; it's really dark back here. You need to make sure I don't fall and hurt myself."

The burning sensation won't leave my face as she tightens her soft fingers and smiles again.

But she has a point—it's much darker on this street than it is on one of the larger Main Streets. That being said, the moon and stars provide plenty of light to see where we're going…

The street gets wider as we make our way out of the backstreets.

What does Aiz think about this…?

I feel ashamed, walking hand in hand with the goddess all this way. Still, I work up the guts to get a glimpse of Aiz's face.

She's wearing her normal emotionless expression. Kind of sad, now that I think about it...

...*Huh?*

Looking at the face of the girl walking next to me, my thought process is a little slow.

Her face is as beautiful as always, but her eyes look sharp, like they're tracking something.

Whoosh.

My head spins around like it's been slapped.

There's a wide path that connects to this backstreet. It's completely shrouded in darkness and so silent that it gives me chills. That kind of complete absence of noise and light is unnatural.

Just as I start to get a bad feeling, my eye catches one of those fancy pole-shaped magic-stone lamps.

...*Someone broke it?*

The pole part hangs from a wooden stand, but the broken light looks like it was hit with something, hard.

"—"

"!"

"Wha—?!"

Aiz freezes in place.

Only she can sense something is wrong at first, but I stop right next to her. The goddess nearly loses her balance in surprise.

Aiz's golden eyes don't try to hide how alert to danger she is right now. I follow her line of sight with my own.

Sure enough, a large shadow emerges from a small space between two buildings.

A cat person...?

The figure blends in with the darkness using black armor, dark clothes, and a black visor over its face.

The visor is made of metal and hiding the top half of the person's face. However, I can see cat ears sticking out of the top of his head. I'm pretty sure it's a man.

Maybe he's the one responsible for the strange aura engulfing this street?

Many questions simmer in my mind as the cat-person adventurer, who stands about a head shorter than me, continues to advance on our position.

There are about two meders left between us when he suddenly plants his foot in the ground.

Thud! A light impact echoes off the stone surface before he vanishes into thin air.

"—"

Less than a breath later, a shadow appears just in front of my face.

Extremely close quarters.

It only took him an instant. His Agility must be off the charts.

My eyes and body shake in response.

Light from the moon sharply reflecting off his metal visor, he silently brings a spear down from above.

Time stops as my life flashes before my eyes.

"—?!"

"?!"

A saber flashes in front of my nose from the side and intercepts the spear just a few celches above my head.

Sparks fly all around me as the thin silver saber pushes the spear back with incredible speed.

Time comes back to me. A fresh wave of cold sweat covers my body, my mind suddenly snaps into action, and I take a fighting stance.

The attacker jumps back to get out of range of Aiz's saber. But the blond girl silently takes another step toward him.

Both of them charge an instant later, colliding in another explosion of sparks.

"W-what…what…*what's going on*?!"

The goddess's panicked screams mix with the sound of metal on metal. The backstreet has turned into a war zone.

—They're too fast!

I'm seeing afterimages of spear arcs and saber slashes, only to hear an impact in a completely different spot.

I can't keep up with them. It's impossible! I can't even follow their movements!

The goddess and I stand to the side and watch as black and golden blurs clash over and over.

"—"

That's when I see them.

Above Aiz's battle with the cat person, four shadows lurk in the darkness.

The shadows leap from the top of the houses, heading straight for the battle.

Sword, whip, spear, axe.

All of them have weapons drawn, glistening dangerously in the moonlight.

"AIZ?!"

Aiz's momentum changes at the same time I call out to her.

Thrusting the cat person away with a long slash, Aiz goes airborne, knocking all the new assailants to the ground with one massive spinning swipe.

My eyes fall open in awe as the metallic echoes of their armor reverberate around me.

"Damn...monster."

Standing at a safe distance from Aiz, the first attacker spits the words out like poison.

"……"

Aiz's saber lightly whistles as she silently makes a few practice swings, letting her sword do the talking.

The five attackers spread out around her, holding their weapons at the ready, and come out of the shadows.

They look like prums. All of them are wearing the same type of armor and visor as the cat person. No doubt about it now—they're working together.

Their trap set, all five of them mercilessly spring at Aiz from all sides.

"B-Bell, let's get out of here. This isn't our stage..."

While the goddess's choice of words sounds a bit like a joke, considering our current situation, she couldn't be more right.

I could never measure up to any of these five attackers—not how I am now, at least. All of them must be top-class adventurers. The speed and precision of their attacks are more than enough evidence.

And in the middle of metallic echoes and sparking chaos stands one blond-haired girl, deflecting the attacks without missing a beat.

She has no room to dodge, but the subtle movements of her sword are inspiring. One sword dances around her, blocking all attacks and finding openings to counterattack. Her strikes find flesh more often than not.

That's the Kenki, the Sword Princess.

Even without being able to see everything in real time, her afterimages show me just how truly *powerful* she is.

Our levels are too far apart.

...I-Idiot!

I know seeing Aiz in action is a bit shocking, but I've been just standing here for far too long.

What am I doing, spacing out at a time like this! Isn't there something that I need to be doing right now?!

If I've got time to stand and watch, I should help her...!

"Wha...?! B-Bell?!"

"?!"

The moment I brace my body to charge into battle, the goddess grabs my shoulder, shrieking at the top of her lungs.

I flip my head around to face her just in time to see four more shadows jump from the rooftops and run to surround us.

Two men, two women. All of them are wearing the same armor and visors as the others.

My eyes tremble.

—What do I do now?

All of the new shadows charge during my moment of indecisiveness.

"!!"

Take them on! I don't have a choice now!

I draw my dagger and the Divine Knife as I launch myself into the four.

"Goddess! Get behind me!"

I engage my first target before hearing an answer.

One of the female attackers is holding a dagger a lot like mine, and she closes the distance in the blink of an eye.

Her visor is hiding her eyes, but I can still sense their aura. She wants to tear me apart. Her blade is coming down!

—I can see it!

She's open on the opposite side of the blade! I quickly step into her space.

"Wh—"

"HA!"

The first blow is mine.

Taking aim at her chest plate, I swing my dagger forward.

Direct hit! My blade hits armor, but the force of the blow sends her flying backward. I don't watch her land as I spin out of the next attack.

Catching the traumatized goddess in my right arm, we avoid a sudden longsword strike. Rolling into the spot that the attack came from to get out of the way, I land a kick to the swordsman's body.

Back on my feet, I use my movement to pivot on my left foot and nail the off-balance swordsman with another kick, before turning to face the other female adventurer. A quick spinning slash and she, too, goes flying.

They're all Level One…!

I'm sure of it.

These guys are small fry compared to the group Aiz is battling right now. They're on my level; the fact that I can see their movement is enough to know that.

There shouldn't be much difference in our statuses at all.

This battle will be won by technique and skill, not power!

Shielding the goddess with my body, I look up to see a heavily armored adventurer lumbering up to us and brace for combat.

"HYAA!!"

Belting out a fierce battle cry, the adventurer swings a thick cleaver down over my head. I bring the Divine Knife up to defend.

Carving a purple arc in the darkness, the Divine Knife slams into the bulk of the cleaver from the side of the blade, at full force.

"Whaa?!"

He sounds surprised. I guess he wasn't expecting me to be able to deflect his attack with a short knife. I use the momentum from the deflection to spin and jump with my right leg and launch a kick that lands square in his face. I'm getting pretty good at this!

"GaaHRK!"

The mountain of metal stumbles backward, dropping the cleaver before falling with a loud crash.

"Bell! The others!"

"!"

The goddess's voice shrieks over the metallic echoes.

They've spread out into a triangle, the goddess and me in the center, all charging at once!

I almost forget to breathe as I make a split-second decision and reach out to grab the cleaver from the street.

"GODDESS! GET DOWN!!"

Her head slides just under the heavy blade as I swing with all my might at the oncoming attackers.

"GaHAA?!"

My first swing with a long, heavy weapon hits all three adventurers in unison, sending them all to the ground with massive damage.

—I used it!

The hilt is uncomfortably large in my hands; my palms feel like they're on fire trying to hold this thing.

"Oooohhh! Bell, that was *so cool*!! I love you again!"

"Please calm down, Goddess!"

In the midst of everything that is happening, I lose my composure for a moment when the goddess jumps onto my chest and wraps her arms around me. But I get my head back up almost immediately.

There is still another battle going on. Countless sparks fly in all directions as Aiz continues her deadly dance of sword and metal.

I know it won't work. But that won't stop me from trying! I raise my right arm and take aim.

Bracing the goddess against my body with my left arm, I watch my targets between my fingers while focusing on my palm.

"AIZ!!"

I see her glance back at me after calling out to her. A swift nod later, she jumps clear of the attackers.

"FIREBOLT!!"

Six blasts in succession.

In less time than it takes to blink, six separate streams of flaming plasma sear the night air on their way toward the men in dark armor.

For a moment, the entire backstreet flashes scarlet.

They hit the targets head-on with a thunderclap, a new wave of sparks erupting on the spot.

But there they are, the cat person and all four prums, standing in a sea of scarlet flames, completely unfazed, before walking out of the fire.

"Magic with no spell…"

"This is worthy news. There is no doubt she will be pleased."

My head prickling and my arm numb after wasting mental energy on a useless attack, the black figures start talking among themselves.

I knew it wouldn't work, but to be completely useless…I feel so small, like I could break at any moment.

Taking quick, short breaths, I slowly lower my arm.

I have never seen the difference between me and top-class adventurers so clearly. There's no comparison…

"Too flashy. This fire will draw too many eyes."

"I realize that……That's enough, withdraw!"

The cat person looked skyward for a moment before issuing that order. All of the rest move at once.

The prums retrieve the adventurers I took down before disappearing once again into the shadows.

All that is left are a few weakening spot fires in the street left over from my Magic.

"Bell..."

"Ah! Excuse me, Goddess..."

I let go of the goddess—she was still pressed against my body by my left arm—giving her a quick apology.

Rather than stepping away, she stays close to me and reaches up to my cheek.

"Are you hurt?"

"......"

Her eyes are full of anxiety as she asks me if I'm okay.

She can probably tell. That makes me even more depressed. More than likely she can see *that*, too.

With the warmth of her soft fingers on the side of my face, I somehow manage to force a smile.

"No injuries?"

"Ah, yes, I'm fine. What about Aiz...?"

"I, too, am fine."

Aiz walks toward us without a scratch on her. Even her face is back to its normal emotionless state.

She just now saved me—heck, she's *always* saving me. I bite my lip and force my brain back to normal to ask a question.

"So who were they? Attacking us out of the blue like that..."

All of their faces were hidden, and I couldn't tell if there was a *Familia* insignia on any of their armor.

Not only did they attack when we were alone, they destroyed the magic-stone lamps as well. Given all that, this was clearly a planned attack with a specific target.

Is there a reason someone would want to ambush us under the cover of darkness...?

"Ambushes happen, all the time."

"They do?!"

"Yes, however it's rare that they happen outside the Dungeon..."

So then this kind of thing is normal in the Dungeon. I'm speechless. I had no idea at all.

And our attackers were at such a high level…They had to belong to an extremely powerful Dungeon-crawling *Familia*.

Is it possible that they knew Aiz was apart from her *Familia* and used this opportunity to attack her…?

"There's something I can't understand. If they were after Wallen-something, that's one thing. But they were after *us*—no, after *you*, Bell."

"Well…"

"On top of that, your attackers were about your level, like they were chosen specifically for you."

…I must admit that the goddess has a very good point.

The ones who fought Aiz would have wiped the floor with me, and yet I could fight and win against the others. Were they set up for me? If I didn't know better, I'd say they were trying to measure me.

That's nothing more than a guess, though…

"Do you know of anyone who would attack you like this, Miss Wallensomething?"

"…Quite the opposite. There are too many."

"Yeesh, Loki's got one dangerous operation going on over there."

"I apologize…"

"Uh…W-well, that doesn't matter. Let's get out of here right now. Someone was bound to hear that explosion and see smoke."

Aiz and the goddess's conversation ends with us deciding to leave this street behind. With everything that's happened, not only will townspeople come to investigate, but some people from the Guild might descend on this spot at any moment.

We need to put some space between us and getting caught up in a bad situation. That's the plan for now.

The goddess takes off at a brisk pace through the thin backstreets. I follow behind her.

That's when I feel it.

"—?!"

Zing! My whole body twitches.

It feels like a hawk snatches my heart out of my chest. But what is this feeling? Am I being watched?

In my mind, I can feel a strange gaze, and a seductive smile.

I look up out of reflex, in the same direction that the cat person had just a moment ago.

There it is: the massive white tower of Babel.

For some reason, my body trembles as the enormous structure looms over me.

"......"

The goddess is busy explaining something to Aiz while the blond girl tilts her head in response. But I stop moving.

Something is coming, I'm sure of it. A black messenger is coming for me.

Beneath a sky of sparkling silver stars, I feel a mysterious rush of cold air blowing from somewhere.

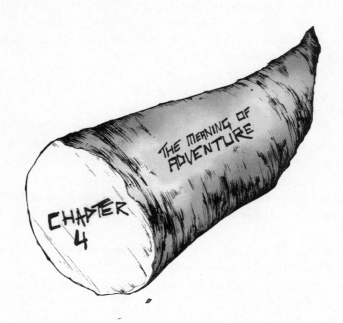

THE MEANING OF ADVENTURE

CHAPTER 4

She nodded to herself.

Aiz sat in an armchair, hugging her knees and deep in thought.

The room she sat in was decorated with light colors and filled with many round tables and sofas. She wasn't alone; many other adventurers were putting their feet up and relaxing in the wide room.

It was the reception room of *Loki Familia*.

"Hey, Aiz. Wha'cha thinking about?"

Aiz lifted her face from between her knees as a wheat-skinned, black-haired girl came up to her.

She had only a strip of cloth around her chest, showing vibrant skin and toned muscles around her midsection. She wore lose, traditional clothing from the waist down. She looked more like a street dancer than an adventurer at the moment.

Aiz made eye contact with the young Amazonian girl sporting a long pareu-style skirt around her waist.

"Tiona..."

"You've had a strange look on your face all week, Aiz. If something's troubling you, I'll help you out!"

Aiz's cheeks warmed as she saw a friendly smile bloom on the young girl's face.

Just as Aiz was opening her mouth to say, "Thank you"...

"Don't even think about it, Aiz. Talkin' ta Tiona ain't gonna solve jack. You'll just get led 'round in circles."

"Get lost, Bete! I'm talking with Aiz, so keep your mouth shut!"

"Kind of sad that Bete has a point, though."

"Not you, too, Tione?! Don't take Bete's side for anything!"

A young animal-person male with ash-gray fur entered the conversation, along with another Amazonian girl.

Bete and Tione walked up to Aiz's armchair, teasing the Amazonian girl along the way.

"But yeah, Aiz, where are ya disappearin' to recently? Nowhere t'be found in the mornings, and yesterday y'were gone all day, weren't ya?"

"What's this? You hear that, Tione? Sounds like Bete's stalking Aiz. Even knows when she's not home. Makes me sick!"

"Quit yer yappin', Amazonian thugs! We're leavin' for an expedition in a few days, and Aiz is out doin' who knows what! That's what I'm sayin' here!"

"It's nothing big, so what's the problem? It's not like she's prowling the Dungeon alone like before. Anything else is a million times safer...and who are *you* calling a thug?!"

Aiz sat quietly, knowing that she was most likely the reason for their argument. However, she also knew that if she spoke up, it would only pour oil on the fire, so she kept her mouth shut.

She watched them argue for a minute before her ears noticed something new close by. She craned her neck to see who was there.

Clack, clack. Two people were playing chess at the table across from her: a tall elf beauty and a short prum boy.

The elf had a head or two of height on the boy, with a very relaxed, almost playful expression on her face, as opposed to the boy's serious face.

"Check."

"Oh..."

The boy moved a piece into position before declaring, which caused the elf's brow to furrow. She still, however, retained her refined beauty despite her arching eyebrows.

Her eyes jumped for a moment as if she thought of something, but she just set her hands on her knees and sighed.

"It's over. I've lost this round."

"That's very sporty of you, Reveria. You could hold out a while longer?"

"I don't like a losing fight, Fynn."

The expression on the prum's face was completely different from the Elf as the two referred to each other by name.

Reveria noticed Aiz's gaze. Her jade hair swayed as she turned to Aiz and asked, "What's wrong?

"Anything we can help you with? I doubt you want to play a round?"

"Ha-ha, Aiz the chess master. Now *that* I'd like to see."

While that got a lighthearted chuckle out of most of the group, the intelligent Fynn softened his lake-blue eyes.

"Tiona asked before, but is something troubling you, Aiz?"

"Wow, that's a first. You can talk with me as well; I'd love to help if I can."

Aiz sat there for a moment after *Loki Familia*'s "top two" leaders asked her if something was wrong. Aiz suddenly started talking, the same thoughtful expression on her face.

"What would the two of you do to teach an adventurer?"

"...Another strange question."

"Hmm. It is interesting to think about, though."

"Eh? What was that? Aiz, what'd you say?!"

The Amazons' argument came to a halt as they joined in.

Both of the girls found a spot close to Aiz's armchair, Bete not far behind.

"That's out of the blue. Aiz, did something happen?"

"When you say 'teach,' you're talking about teaching an adventurer weaker than yourself, yes?"

"No need. You'd be wasting your time, tryin' ta teach a bottom-feeder. Don't be stupid."

Aiz still hugged her knees to her chest as her comrades formed a circle around her. She decided to ask everyone at once.

"What would anyone do?"

"I would guide them through meditation. No one can improve without knowing themselves first."

"Oh? I'd bring them with me to the Dungeon! Nothing like a baptism of fire to get results!"

"Sparring, I believe. Get them used to the rough and tumble of battle."

"Tiona, isn't that exactly what sparring means?"

The ladies of the group each said their opinions in turn, but Bete scoffed at them, snorting out his nose.

"Don't make me repeat myself! Bottom-feeders belong at the bottom. As long as they're weak, there's no point in teachin' 'em anything!"

"...Bete, that's very philosophical of you."

"Hah! He's just trying to act tough!"

"I'll bite you in half, woman...!"

"On the other hand, those with power shouldn't think too much of themselves and show their techniques without a purpose...I never thought I would learn something such as this from Bete."

"You wanna get in line, old hag...?"

Aiz watched as the conversation broke off into several parts. She turned to face the last person yet to speak, Fynn.

"What about you, Fynn?"

"Hmm, what would I do? For starters, I'd like to figure out what my student's weaknesses are, and from there figure out a way to make them into strengths. But getting that far seems difficult."

Fynn scratched his chin as his small frame sank deeper and deeper into the sofa.

He then answered Aiz's question with a question.

"Why do you ask, Aiz? Your answer will likely affect mine."

"...I..."

The reason for her question was simple.

She was trying to figure out the best way to instruct a certain boy.

It had been six days since she offered to become his teacher. At first she wanted to find the cause of his rapid growth, but now she was curious to see just how much he could improve.

Aiz herself didn't understand why she was so motivated to come up with a "menu" for their next lesson, but Bell's desire to get stronger was a definite factor.

He was open and honest, in a good way.

More than likely he would bravely take everything Aiz might throw at him, enduring and learning from Aiz's strict lessons, no matter how tough.

Since he never complained, and faced all situations head-on, he learned quickly.

Not that he was particularly good at learning—just quick to recover. Every time he failed, he just lined up and tried again.

So that's why Aiz has been racking her brain these last few days. To teach him the best way she could, and to reward him for his efforts.

Right now, she was his only example.

If Fynn were to figure this out, there might be problems...

However, even if there were a better way, she couldn't let her connection with Bell come to light.

And then there was the incident the previous night, when she was away from her *Familia*—a mysterious group (Aiz could only think of one "group" with members that powerful) had attacked her under the cover of darkness.

To keep her interaction with Bell under wraps, she also had to keep the night raid a secret.

"...was curious about it. Yes."

"...Okay, then. In that case, this is my conclusion."

Fynn's golden hair slightly shook as he tilted his head.

He gathered his thoughts before speaking.

"There are times when we as adventurers must go on adventures. Imparting the mental toughness to face that time without fear onto a student would be the best, I think."

Aiz listened well to her ally's words, taking them to heart. She gave a heartfelt "Thank you" in response.

Stretching his shoulders, Fynn slowly got to his feet.

"While I want to avoid doing something careless, I think this is a good opportunity for you, Aiz. Whatever group you've made a connection with, don't stop now. I don't know how long I'll be able to play stupid, but I'll keep this a secret from Loki as long as possible."

"……"

"However, I won't hesitate to tell her if I think your actions are putting our *Familia* in danger. Let's leave it at that."

Fynn smiled one last time before leaving the reception room. Aiz silently watched him go.

She now knew that she couldn't lie to either Reveria or the prum leader of the *Familia*; they could both see right through her.

"But you know, Aiz, it seems like you're having a good time."

"......Having a good time?"

Tiona had broken away from the rest of the group and come up to Aiz's chair.

Aiz looked confused. Tiona simply nodded.

"When you're not in the Dungeon, you usually just space out or practice with your saber. But now you're nodding to yourself, trying your hardest to figure something out. I can see that much."

The Amazonian girl's toothy grin reflected off Aiz's golden eyes.

"Thinking about something, realizing something, trying something...You look like you're enjoying yourself."

"...Maybe that's true."

"Yes, it is. You're having fun, Aiz."

The girl hit the nail right on the head as she confidently told Aiz how she looked.

Aiz smiled happily to herself.

Everything around me sounds distant.

A wave of shock tears through my motionless body as my eyes are locked on a piece of paper in my hands. The paper is still pinned to the wall.

Words escape my mouth.

"Level six......"

The paper is a list of public level announcements of all adventurers, strongest at the top. My spirit leaves my body the moment my eyes find the name Aiz Wallenstein.

"It was very recent. We only got news of Miss Wallenstein's rank a few days ago..."

Eina's words pass through one ear and out the other.

The shock of seeing that the person I'm trying with all my might to catch up to just put even more space between us makes my head go numb. It feels like I'm on earth and she's somewhere in the clouds.

I came by the Guild Headquarters on my way home from the Dungeon.

I don't normally look at the notice board in the Guild lobby, but I happened to catch a glimpse of it on my way by and asked Eina if it was true.

"According to my sources, she slew a floor boss on her own. Not in the Lower Fortress of the Dungeon, but in the even lower Deep Zone..."

Floor boss...Monster Rex.

By far the most powerful monster on their floor, it takes large groups of adventurers to take one down.

Far outclassing all other monsters in strength and size, defeating a Monster Rex is supposed to be the most difficult part of conquering a floor.

In fact, a *Familia* can be defined by how many of its members have been involved in a successful battle against one of those gargantuan beasts. There aren't many that have even slain one...

And she did it alone...?

"Um...Bell. This might be difficult for you, but you shouldn't think about this too hard. Even I've never heard of anyone slaying a floor boss alone before. Miss Wallenstein is...special."

It's probably just as she says.

Even still, that doesn't stop my spirit from sinking into oblivion.

What she did in that backstreet the other night is still on replay in my mind.

I can see her facing down five of the strongest adventurers in the city without so much as a step backward, the flashes of her blade, the sudden bursts of sparks, the clash of steel on steel.

I learned just how insignificant I am on that night, watching that battle between masters.

Fast.

They're too fast.

Just how much stronger is she, compared to me?

Can I even hope to reach that high...? Way up in the clouds?

The cold, hard truth had taken hold of my soul, and is crushing it to pieces.

"Bell...?"

"...Ah, sorry. Kind of spaced out for a minute there. I'm going home."

Eina looks worried, so I do my best to smile at her and bow my head to be polite.

We exchange a few more words like "Good luck tomorrow" and "See you again soon" before I turn to make my exit.

Eina sees me off, waving with a very uncertain look on her face.

I'll put on a strong face, but...

I'm floored.

The way my depressed body is walking, I'll probably trip over every stone in the street.

Loosing sigh after sigh, I walk with my head down, staring at my feet as I make my way down Main Street.

The sun is setting in the western sky. The lower it gets, the livelier the street becomes. The bars are open, drawing in customers one by one. I can hear a harp playing—that's new. It looks like an elf, and he's singing in a beautiful timbre about the brave, powerful adventurers of Orario.

I stop to listen, and he smiles at me. I didn't know what to do, so I smile back and give him a few coins out of my pocket before making a quick escape...Some powerful, brave adventurer I am.

Rather than going straight home, I double back and go into Central Park. Waves of adventurers are coming out of Babel Tower, out of the Dungeon. But I'm just killing time. After a while I decide to head back to West Main.

I don't feel like I'm part of this town; the noise of the street has nothing to do with me.

"—Bell!"

"Huh?"

I take my eyes off the street and look for the source of the voice that suddenly calls out to me.

Swishing blue-gray hair is running toward me. Syr?

Have I already come as far as The Benevolent Mistress?

Just as I start recognizing some of the taverns in the area, Syr grabs my hand without warning.

"Huh...?"

"......"

Both of her hands grasp my right, her smooth, milky-white skin against mine.

I'm lost for words as she lifts up my hand, looking at it. It's like she's saying me she caught me, but she's enjoying the warmth of my hand, too.

My face is getting redder and redder. She looks up to meet my eyes, a very happy smile on her face, and says these words:

"Bell, I've been looking for you...!"

"......"

Clatter, clatter. The sounds of running water and dishes fill my ears, steam in my face as I work my way through a never-ending stack of them.

The cat-people chefs are busily running around the kitchen while I quietly wash dishes in a corner, alone.

"I really appreciate this, Bell! To think you'd volunteer to help me at work!"

"I didn't *volunteer* to do anything! You practically forced me!"

She stopped her trotting feet to give me a light bow of apology as I yelled back with enough force to send spit flying out of my mouth.

I said I'd come with her for a little while when we ran into each other outside, but washing dishes isn't exactly what I had in mind.

"I ignored a lot of chores and went out this morning...That made Mama Mia really mad at me, and now I've got so much more to do than before!"

"That is completely one hundred percent your problem!"

Didn't she just say "went out" after "ignoring chores"?!

But then again, she *is* running around like a madwoman, so I guess she really is busy.

Weaving her way in and out of other waitresses, Syr is taking care of odd jobs all over the bar and kitchen.

"Meow, this is a surprise, White Head."

"Enslaved by Syr, meow. His duty, meow!"

"Ugh…"

Doing my best to take the teasing of the cat-girl waitresses Ahnya and Chloe in stride, I continue attacking the white mountain of plates next to the sink.

Of course I'm not very happy with this…But the people here have helped me out so many times before, and Syr is still making lunches for me, so why not do her a favor?

But why did it have to be washing dishes? I scream inside my head as I continue to fill in for Syr.

"…"

Then again, having an endless-seeming task to do might be the best thing for me right now.

The constant movement and the noise back here are keeping my mind off of *her*, after all.

I keep my mouth closed as I continue whipping down dish after dish.

"Are you okay, Mr. Cranell?"

"Huh…?"

"This amount is daunting. I shall assist."

Now I have a guest—another bar employee next to me at the sink.

Arms so thin they seem like they're about to break set to work next to me. The girl's long, thin ears flash in my vision.

An elf with light blue eyes, deep as the sky itself, looks up at me. It's Lyu.

"S-sorry. I know you're busy, too…"

"No, the situation is Syr's fault. And blame also lies with us, the employees who couldn't cover for her. We owe you the apology. On behalf of all of us, allow me to convey our apologies."

"No-no-no-no, you don't have to go that far!"

I stop washing for a moment to face the always-serious Lyu, who's almost *too* serious right now, and respond to her. I know she's very conscious of manners and protocol, but this is a whole new level of correctness.

Whatever it is, Lyu must be a great example of elfish integrity.

"Has something happened?"

"Eh—"

"I don't mean to be forward, but you appear to be depressed."

I stand next to her in shocked silence as her hands fly around the sink, washing the dishes with amazing precision.

Elves are known for their good looks. Lyu is no exception. Even just looking at her profile, she's a radiant beauty with a bit of a cold aura. It's enough to make me nervous standing this close to her.

"If you consider me worthy, I'll listen."

"…"

"I owe you for your assistance at this station. If you have no reservations, please allow me to help."

Honestly, standing here and admiring her beauty like this, part of me wants to tell her everything about anything.

But no, I can't do that. I don't want to.

I can't tell her that the person I idolize has left me in the dust and exposed just how weak and pathetic I am. There's still some sorry piece of me that has hope that I can catch up to *her* by trying harder.

It feels a bit cowardly, but I decide to ask Lyu about something else instead.

After hearing that Aiz had leveled up earlier today, there's something I'd like to know.

"Um, Lyu…Were you an adventurer?"

"…Yes. There was a time I was known as one. What are you getting at?"

I quickly explain to her that I'm not trying to find out about her past, before asking my question.

"It's about getting stronger…How does an adventurer level up?"

I've always thought that if I continue fighting and gaining excelia I'd rank up eventually, but that doesn't seem to be the case.

The difference between Level One and Level Two...It feels like there's a wall between them. A very steep wall, one that I have to climb over if I'm ever going to level up.

Lyu listened to my question, her eyes on me. She opens her mouth to respond.

"You must do something great."

"...Huh?"

"You must complete a great task, something that even the gods cannot ignore."

Great...?

"Defeat an enemy more powerful than yourself...Acquire an incredible amount of excelia in one shot. That is the requirement."

Gaining a large amount of excelia all at once...So that means no matter how many lower-level monsters I slay, I'll never rank up. Only my basic stats will improve.

If I don't take down something really powerful, if I don't pull off something great like the hero in *Tales of Adventure*...I'll never reach her?

"An adventurer's level is the strength of their soul—a 'container' within them. A god's blessing allows the soul to grow, but only those who have proven themselves deserving."

"Well, what about my abilities? My basic stats...?"

"In short, they are there to prepare you to do something great. Nothing more."

But they are also qualifications.

Lyu goes on to tell me that an adventurer can level up once all their basic stats are above D.

"But fighting a monster that's more powerful than you are... doesn't that mean you'd lose?"

That's what "stronger than you" means, right?

"Overcoming that disadvantage is part technique and part strategy...I'll tell you a common way to overcome it: form a battle party."

"A party?"

"Yes. Using combined strength and strategy to slay a beast

stronger than any of the party members. Adventurers in Orario repeat this many times to get stronger."

Sounds like the excelia would be split between all party members, but it's a fool-proof way for a weakling to become powerful.

"Mr. Cranell, if you truly wish to become stronger, a battle party is required. Please keep this in mind."

"Okay…"

But that means that *she*…

She took down a floor boss, slew a monster of that size and strength, on her own—such heights are…

Feeling trapped by just how high my goal is, it reminds me just how far up top-class adventurers really are.

"…I have advice to offer you. Is this acceptable?"

"Ah, yes. Go ahead."

Lyu's voice brings me out of my reverie. She starts talking.

"Mr. Cranell. Every adventure has a meaning."

"……"

"No one knows what awaits them on an adventure. However, do not lose sight of the meaning of setting out, the purpose."

Pausing for a moment to give me a chance to think about her words, she continues.

"You are an adventurer."

Her words plunge into my ears and make their way to the bottom of my soul.

"What you seek, most likely, cannot be obtained without venturing forward."

"U-um…"

"But no, please don't worry about it. My intuition is often wrong."

For a second there, I think she smiles at me. I blink quickly to clear my eyes, and she's wearing her usual cold expression.

I rub my eyes, just to make sure. She asks me if I'm all right; I wave it off and say it's nothing.

After that, the two of us manage to conquer the beast that is the mountain of dirty dishes.

"Well then, Mr. Cranell. Please visit us again when you have an opportunity."

"Sure, I'll drop by again soon."

Lyu has more to do, so she sees me out of the kitchen as I walk through the door into the main bar of The Benevolent Mistress. The bar is alive with voices, busy as usual. I look out onto the café terrace for a moment before making my way to the exit. It's time to go home.

"Bell."

"…Syr."

I turn around to the voice that called me, and there she is, standing right in front of me.

Her white cheeks are pinkish, and I wonder if it has something to do with finishing the job she dragged me into.

"I'm really sorry about today…Thank you so much for your help."

"Ah, well, I said a few things at first, but you've helped me out many times, too…"

My words come out a bit clumsily because she's bowing to me. Her usual hair bun with a ponytail sticking out the middle is right in front of my face.

I can't exactly tell her off when she's like this; it's like an aggressive apology.

Not that I really need one.

"…Bell."

"……?"

She raises her head and looks me square in the eyes.

Her lips open, close, open again. But there's no sound. Is she trying to tell me something? I tilt my head in confusion.

"I'm not an adventurer, so I don't really know how to put this…"

"Syr?"

"…But you don't have to go on adventures, right?"

My eyes open wide as her soft voice reaches my ears.

She breaks off eye contact, looking over her shoulder and forcing a smile.

"Please don't do anything reckless. That's what I'm trying to say."

© Suzuhito
Yasuda

"......"

"...To think I'd lose my nerve, now of all times."

I've never seen her like this. It looks like she's got a lot of weight on her shoulders as she whispers those words under her breath.

Did she hear my conversation with Lyu?

She's just a civilian, so some things in that conversation might have been a little shocking.

"Sorry, that must have sounded weird."

"No, no..."

"I'll always have a lunch prepared for you. Please keep coming from now on."

A nervous smile comes to my lips as I suddenly understand the true meaning of her words.

To make sure that the day when I don't come will never arrive, it's her way of warning me.

She gives me one last beautiful smile, still in her waitress uniform, before turning around and getting back to work.

"......"

With warm, orange light coming out of the windows and the happy voices of customers spilling out the front door, I look up at the night sky.

It feels like I've hit a fork in the road.

On one side is the path the Lyu has set before me. The other one has been suggested by Syr—and also Eina, now that I think about it.

—*You are an adventurer.*

—*Adventurers must not go on adventures.*

They are maybe, probably, complete opposites, for sure.

I do my best to clear my mind and let their words stew for a moment.

Unable to choose a path at this fork in the road, I keep staring at the stars in the black sky.

The first sunbeams of the morning burst over the horizon, lighting up the top of Orario's city wall.

The mountain range in the distances lights up in a flash as I feel the sun's warmth on the side of my face.

It's almost over.

I'm still in the middle of a fierce training session, but I know.

The girl with the blond hair launches an endless barrage of merciless attacks.

This is the task she has given me: while being peppered by blow after blow of her sheath, to move my body to protect the targeted area.

That, and block the sheath.

My eyes catch glimpses of her attacks as I have steadily increased the number of blocked attacks since early this morning.

There's a technique I've seen her do hundreds of times, her defensive trump card.

Rather than block an enemy attack head-on, redirect the weapon's path by hitting it from the side and let the blade travel harmlessly away from your body.

After everything that's happened, how hard I've tried up until first sun on the last day, it's time for me to use it against her.

"—!!"

I move my feet into a safe position, take a deep breath, and face her attack head-on.

Shifting my weight, weaving through the onslaught, I dodge some blows and redirect others before seeing an opening to slash with the dagger in my right hand.

Then.

I drop my guard and go on the offensive for the first time.

"......!"

The sound of metal on metal.

Her armor easily deflected my attack. But it hit.

I let my arm fall, breathing heavily as the girl, Aiz, looked at me in silence.

The sun clears the mountains, bathing our stage in soft morning light. I squint as my eyes adjust.

But in that moment, she smiles. It's not that I can see it at the other end of the light, but I can feel it.

"This is the end..." Aiz quietly says as she looks at me.

Part of the sun is visible in the eastern sky from where we're standing on the top of the city wall. It's the sign that this week and our training sessions are over.

I watched the city light up below me for a moment. Once I realize Aiz is watching the same thing, our eyes meet. I lower my head.

"Thank you, for everything."

I bend my waist into a deep bow and look at the stone path once again.

Thinking back on this week, it may have been short, but every moment felt like a dream come true.

I straighten my back and make eye contact once again with Aiz. She's wearing her usual aloof expression, but her eyes seem soft as she replies in a warm voice:

"Thanks, from me too. This was...fun."

The golden sunlight shines on her face, brightening her golden eyes as her lips form the first true smile I've ever seen her make.

Even now, on the last moment of the last day, I blush in front of her. I try to respond, opening and closing my mouth a few times before giving up and nodding a few times.

"...Well then, do your best."

"...I will."

Leaving those words, she slowly turns and walks away.

As I watch her disappear in the light, the only thought in my mind is: Will I ever be able to reach her?

Will there ever be another moment like the one before, where I get close enough to reach out and touch her?

If there's one thing I've learned this week, it's that my path to her is an extremely long one.

Long enough to make me stop in awe and even fall into despair.

Is it really possible for someone like me to catch up to that girl walking away?

"......"

But I have to try.

If I don't try, I've already failed. Failed before I even start.

The possibility of standing next to her, of catching her is gone if I don't try.

Getting to her level, that incredible height...touching that shoulder. I have to reach out once again.

I may be a weakling right now, but I swear to the rising sun I will reach her one day.

After taking one last look at her flowing blond hair, I turn my back and sprint in the opposite direction.

Eina organized all the paperwork strewn out on her desk and sighed.

Many of her coworkers had finished their work for the day and were getting ready to leave.

The clock close to the ceiling on the wall facing her read eight o'clock in the evening. They were in the office section in the corner of the Guild lobby. Since only people working overtime were still there, the Guild itself felt very empty.

Just as Eina thought about going and getting a cup of coffee, she heard the pouting voice of her friend and coworker in the same department.

"Heeh, Eina, a little help—! I can't finish this all alone by morning?!"

"...You reap what you sow. You've done nothing about those documents until this afternoon, Misha. It's your fault."

Misha's whine did nothing to convince Eina to reconsider her refusal.

The human Guild employee named Misha returned to her desk, which was lined with enough paperwork to rival Orario's city wall.

They have piled up this much because her continued neglect of requests to post information from the gods and goddesses of various *Familias* around Orario.

"Just why the heck are so many adventurers leveling up at once?!

A last-minute level-up rush?! This is insane! Someone's got it in for me...!"

"Hey, none of that! That's the result of many adventurers' sweat and blood on your desk, and all you do is complain. If you'd taken care of a little bit each day, this wouldn't have happened, yes?"

"Yes, I'm repenting, Eina, repenting...! So please help me, Eina?!"

"N-O."

Eina turned her back to make her point final. She sighed after Misha's final appeal: "Why are you so heartless?!" Eina thought it might be a good idea to bring her coworker some coffee as well.

"......"

Feeling the effects of a long day's work, Eina moved her right hand from her elbow to her chin as she looked down at the document she had just finished writing.

It was an application for approval to formally investigate the internal affairs of *Soma Familia*.

It contained information that she had gathered personally from both Bell and the Goddess Loki herself.

However, Eina was not trying to disband *Soma Familia*. Of course she had her own thoughts about how that *Familia* was operating—plenty of them.

If talk of disbanding the *Familia* came up, the supporter whom Bell had mentioned, Lilly, would have to be punished, from a strictly just standpoint. No matter the extenuating circumstances, there would be some kind of punishment.

Eina was not some kind of goddess of justice; she had no sword or scales to wield.

She had half a mind not to get involved; this wasn't her fight.

But this was something more than that for her.

If she could make something better for adventurers—anything at all—by bringing circumstances to light, then she had no problem overstepping her bounds to do so.

Eina wished for nothing more than the safe return of all adventurers, and she was willing to get burned in the process, to make sure that came to pass.

There was no turning back after I got involved with that Familia...

Eina knew just how much personal information was in this document, and that she was incriminating herself by writing it.

That *Familia*...Bell's *Familia*.

In the end, her desire to help Bell was what convinced her to go to *Loki Familia*, and ultimately get involved with the problems in *Soma Familia*.

This was something that a Guild employee—someone who was supposed to be neutral and in the background at all times—should never have done. Her actions were completely different from simply giving Bell advice and leaving it at that.

It was an abuse of power, as well as cause for her removal from the Guild.

However.

...Ignoring this situation is much worse.

Even if it meant failing in her duties as a Guild employee, it was much better to follow through with this than fail as the person, Eina Tulle. It might have been flawed logic, but her mind was already made up.

The same noble blood that flowed within Reveria also flowed within her. She might be only half-elf, but she didn't want to do anything to disgrace her name or kin.

If I do get dismissed...Perhaps I should try to join Hestia Familia.

Telling herself a joke to keep her spirits up, Eina thought about her options for a new place of employment.

As she chuckled to herself, Eina's shoulder-length brown hair lightly swished around her neck.

"What is it, Eina? You sure are grinning all of a sudden."

"I'm not *grinning*. Don't exaggerate."

"Yeah, yeah, but really. Did something happen? Tell me, tell me!"

"Nothing major...I was just thinking about my next job..."

"Next job...No way! You're quitting the Guild?!"

Slide, scrape, slide. The moment Misha raised her voice in surprise, half of their coworkers jumped out of their seats—the male half.

Feeling the sudden pressure of many sets of eyes trained on her, Eina quickly corrected her friend's misunderstanding.

"N-no, no. Just thinking about 'if I were to be fired,' that's all. I have no intention of quitting the Guild."

"Don't scare me like that…And there's no way you'll be canned, Eina."

*That's not entirely true…*Eina thought, and forced a smile.

Meanwhile, the men who stood up let out a small "Oh" in unison and sat back down.

In any case…

Once she turned in this document, an investigation into Soma's managing policies would be under way.

Even though there was no problem with the group itself, many of its members had been flirting with the darkest side of the gray zone. Considering the information in Bell's testimony, it was almost guaranteed that some of them would be punished for crimes against civilians.

There were cases in which entire *Familias* had been banished from Orario for ignoring the Guild's warnings.

For a god who was only interested in his hobby, like Soma, a warning like this ought to be enough for him to reconsider some of his policies.

And it turns out the supporter named Erde wasn't a bad prum, after all…

Eina had tracked down and visited the elderly couple who'd gotten caught up in Lilly's issue with *Soma Familia*. They told her what happened after that horrible day, with a tinge of guilt in their voices.

Ever since they kicked her out, money started appearing in front of their store. Since it came on a consistent basis, they never filed a damage report to the Guild.

They asked Eina to apologize to Lilly in their place, but Eina refused. It was the elderly couple's duty to tell Lilly directly, no one else's.

...The sweat and blood of adventurers, eh.

Eina remembered the words she had spoken only minutes ago.

She looked up, as if looking far off into the distance.

If adventurers trample others under their feet...then some of that sweat and blood doesn't belong to the adventurers, does it?

Not all of it, anyway, Eina thought.

Eina earnestly hoped that all adventurers would make it home every day, and wanted to support them. But there was one thing that made her question herself: the adventurers who were able to commit such atrocities without so much as batting an eye.

Her own emotions contradicted each other; a very strange feeling. This wasn't the first time that Eina had questioned whether or not she was doing the right thing by supporting adventurers. Eina's body shuddered where she stood.

She knew that she was overthinking it, but that didn't stop a twinge of uneasiness from flowing through her.

"...Tulle."

"Ah, yes?"

The call of one of her coworkers brought her out of her reverie before she could find an answer.

A man whose desk was close to the reception counter waved his hand and pointed toward the lobby.

Eina looked in that direction in time to see Bell walking toward the counter.

"...Thank you."

She did a quick bow and left her desk.

Her face had been rather dark, but now a small ray of light had broken through.

Eina quickened her pace and met Bell out in the lobby.

...But there are also adventurers out there giving it everything they've got.

Bell smiled when he saw Eina emerge from behind the counter.

Eina smiled back at him.

Of course there were many kinds of adventurer, but seeing their passion and ability to ignore inconsequential things made Eina happy.

While there might have been adventurers willing to abandon a supporter, there were also adventurers willing to save a supporter.

If it was to help them, Eina felt like getting fired or depressed was worth it. Her wish for adventurers to stay alive was pure.

Eina realized it as she looked at the rather diminutive adventurer standing before her.

It's been said that the good ones die young, while the bad live on...

Eina didn't believe this, however; she didn't want to. But she could do her best to keep the good ones alive.

It was time for that "superstition" to come to an end.

This was the Labyrinth City, Orario.

A city with a will of its own where even the gods didn't know what would happen next.

Kanu froze on the spot.

"K-KANU?! HELP ME—GYA!!"

He could only stand and watch blood burst out of the other adventurer's body.

"GYUAAAAHH...!"

Bloodred, mad bull.

A fresh wave of the red liquid ran down its toned, two-meder-tall body as it looked up to the high ceiling, before unleashing an explosion from its vocal cords.

"UWOOOOOHHHHHHHHH!!"

A monstrous howl.

Kanu's ears bled, his body still frozen with fear as he came crashing down on his rear end.

With muscles like boulders, the beast's entire body looked like a weapon. Far less could strike real fear into the hearts of many adventurers.

A Minotaur.

It was a name given to this type of monster, but this particular example wielded a large cleaver as it hacked and slashed its way through adventurers one by one.

This all started when Kanu happened across a group of Amazons fighting against a giant of a man.

Their heated battle covered well over half of a wide room. It was a battle between masters, adventurers who were far too powerful to waste time in the upper floors of the Dungeon. The battle that unfolded in front of Kanu's eyes was beyond epic.

At first, Kanu and his battle party couldn't believe their eyes as they watched the attackers gang up on the solo adventurer, but after noticing the emblem on the beast person's armor—the profile of a goddess surrounded by a golden necklace—they realized this was a battle between members of the same *Familia*.

The mountain of a man belonged to *Freya Familia*. As the goddess of love and beauty, Freya had many enemies based on that alone. The power of jealousy knows no bounds.

So it was only natural that her enemies would try to get back at her in any way possible. Freya herself didn't seem worried by the fact that her adventurers were often targeted when they traveled alone in the Dungeon.

While it was still unknown to Kanu and his group, rumors that this man, Ottar, was prowling around the seventeenth level for the past week had been circulating for some time now. This attack on Ottar was all part of a goddess's plan to keep things interesting.

These combatants were far out of their league. Kanu and his compatriots could only gawk at them from a safe distance. That is, until someone noticed something peculiar.

The beast person was completely ignoring the difference in numbers, instead choosing to protect a large cargo box behind him.

That was the moment of truth.

Kanu and his battle party circled around behind the battle and waited for an opportunity to steal it. Once they made their move, all they heard behind them were the sounds of combat. Kanu was confident that Ottar had to fend off too many attackers to pursue them immediately.

They raced through the Dungeon with the cargo box in tow. That being said, it was slow going due to the size and weight of the box, but they needed to get as far away from Ottar as they could, as quickly as possible.

Kanu was convinced that this cargo box was full of loot from the lower Dungeon—the hard-fought gains of a top-class adventurer. The magic sword that he'd recently *acquired* from a...former associate of his was fresh in his mind, and Kanu had no doubt that his good luck would continue.

Then.

Once they had put enough distance between themselves and the beast man, Kanu and his party lost their patience and decided to divvy up the loot right then and there.

That's when they saw exactly what was inside.

A bound and extremely angry Minotaur.

Without exception, every member of that battle party's minds went blank.

It wasn't long until red filled their eyes.

The Minotaur ripped the chains that restricted its hands clean off in a rage, crushing one of Kanu's allies into a pulp in the process.

Letting out a howl that signaled the end of the world, the enraged Minotaur emerged from the cargo box with fresh blood on its hands.

"Hyeeaah...yaaaaahh?!"

A man—one of the last survivors of his battle party—let out a scream that sounded no better than a broken flute as he ran in circles.

The normally grassy floor had become a bloody marsh. His battle party was nothing more than fertilizer now, part of the gruesome field of death. The room had become an abattoir.

However, the man had lost the ability to think rationally and ran himself into a corner trying to escape.

The Minotaur advanced on the human at a leisurely pace, its eyes locked onto the back of the adventurer's exposed neck.

Kanu looked over his shoulder to see an extremely unnatural sight: the Minotaur carrying a massive cleaver that happened to be in the cargo box, as if the monster were an adventurer.

"I-It's a dead end...?!"

"Mroooooooo...!"

"Yaaaagh?!"

Understanding the part his ally had to play in this episode, Kanu could only smile.

Neither his body posture nor his expression changed, only the color of his face as he watched the beast approach the man.

"Hrrrrnnn...!"

"Why, damn it all! Why are you here?!" The human screamed with his back to the wall. The Minotaur looked down on him, its shoulders heaving with each breath.

This Minotaur listened to its instincts and raised the cleaver as the whimpering human shrank to the floor.

All of the beast's muscles tightened in rhythm, raising the blade high like a guillotine.

A dark shadow fell over the human adventurer, pure despair filling his mind.

The man's wordless screams of panic and fear filled the room until—

"Mooooooooh!!!"

Thok. The sound of a slicing impact shot through the room, accompanied by the beast's ferocious howl.

SPLASH. Yet another wave of fresh blood ran down the monster's body.

"...Huh?"

Only able to see the beast's shoulders from his vantage point, Kanu couldn't see exactly what had become of his former party member.

But he only needed to look at the red splatter of blood and guts on the wall to know all that he needed to.

© Suzuhito Yasuda

Kanu stood there in shock, a sitting duck out in the open, as the smallest of sounds fell out of his mouth.

"Mroo—"

But it was enough for the Minotaur to hear him.

The Minotaur turned, its face still contorted by rage.

Its eyes, surrounded by a splatter of fresh blood, shot through Kanu like hot knives into butter.

The adventurer's body stiffened, as if chains had enveloped him from the inside out. Kanu started to hyperventilate.

"Mroooooooo!!"

He ran.

Breaking free of his mental chains, he put so much power into his first steps that he nearly fell flat on his face.

Regaining his balance, Kanu ran as fast as he could, the echoes of the beast's roar right on his heels.

He was moving so fast that his boots sounded like whips as they hit the floor, his eyes wide. His mind was beginning to leave him.

The hideous god of death was catching up.

You've got to be kidding—?!

His breath was ragged, panting like a rapid dog. His thoughts were going all over the place, but none of his thoughts came to any kind of conclusion.

It was as if his mind was boiling inside his own head. Hot, much too hot.

Rivers of sweat flowed from his body as he sprinted like a madman.

Kanu had been running without much thought to where he was going. He nearly lost his balance many times, focusing only on making his escape.

It was nighttime outside the Dungeon. There were no other adventurers prowling these halls. He was truly alone in the Dungeon. It had become an endless labyrinth where the same walls and patterns went on into eternity.

Can't shake it, can't shake it, can't shake it......?!

He couldn't escape the overwhelming presence that was just behind him.

This wasn't right. The beast's aura was drowning him in his own fear.

Minotaurs were supposed to be known for their head-on bull-rush attacks, or so Kanu screamed at nothing in particular as he tried to put some space between himself and the monster.

Half of one of the Minotaur's horns was missing, broken off by something else. It was as if through that pain, the beast gained intelligence.

The Minotaur held the cleaver in its right hand, giving chase with all speed.

"Haa-ha-haahaa?!"

Kanu gasped for breath as he made a sudden change of course, throwing his body into a small side path.

Desperate to go forward, desperate for distance.

All semblance of calm gone, the man wished for nothing more than a release from the fear that consumed him.

He had absolutely no idea where he was or how he got there.

His boots treaded grass as he prayed for the speed to escape death.

Before he knew it, he'd run himself into a room with no exit.

"Son of a—?!"

His eyes nearly jumped out of their sockets.

His voice sounded tight, like his vocal cords were seconds from snapping.

Once he realized what had happened, Kanu turned around with his eyes shaking.

The thundering footsteps that had been chasing him were gone. It was a moment of silence so thick it was suffocating.

The next moment, out of nowhere…

The half-horned Minotaur stuck its face out from around the corner.

"—?!"

A scream to end all screams rocketed out of Kanu's ragged throat.

He had crossed the line from fear into sheer terror. Panic flooded his body.

The Minotaur fully emerged, gripping the cleaver in its powerful grasp. The massive sword would require two hands and an incredible amount of strength for a normal person to wield. However, in the hands of the Minotaur, it looked like nothing more than a longsword designed to be held in one hand.

Savage breath passed through intimidating, sharp white teeth.

Its dripping red weapon and bloodshot eyes were starving for another kill.

"G-get away!"

Kanu reached behind his back and pulled out a crimson knife.

Aiming the magic blade at the slowly oncoming monster, he waved it frantically until its power was unleashed.

"GUWOU......!"

"Go! Scram! Get the hell away from me!"

The flames that shot forward from the magic blade hit their target head-on.

Kanu shook the blade with all of his might; volley after volley of flames found their mark. With nowhere to run, this wall of fireballs was the only thing between him and certain death.

The Minotaur shielded itself from the onslaught with one of its huge arms. Kanu launched round after round after round...That is, until he heard a loud *crack*. The blade fell to pieces in his hand.

"Haa...whaaa?!"

The now lifeless magic blade had reached its limit, crumbling into smaller and smaller pieces as it fell to the ground.

The adventurer somehow managed a scream of surprise as his last line of defense fizzled out.

At the end of it all, Kanu was betrayed by his own weapon.

"Hnfff, hnfff...!!"

"Eeee-eeeeeeee!!"

Sparks still smoldering in its blood-soaked fur, the Minotaur had come close enough for Kanu to smell the beast's putrid breath.

Enraged eyes bore into him.

The Minotaur's muscles tightened as its shadow on the wall, and it raised its sword high.

"N-nooooo—!"

Kanu's consciousness disappeared into oblivion with a crushing, splitting pain in the center of his head.

Crack!

The handle of a mug broke off.

"......"

Hestia stopped moving, her gaze snapping to the spot.

The white mug broke on its own, the separated white handle teetering on its back like a seesaw.

It was a clean break; the mug had become a handle-less cup.

"......"

Hestia stood there quietly, staring at the former mug, feeling uneasy. This kind of a break wasn't normal. The sound of hurried footsteps and heavy clothing made her turn her head in time to see Bell walk past the table.

He had just finished his training with Aiz. Whether he was anxious to put his new skills to the test or not, he seemed like he was in more of a hurry than usual to get an early start in the Dungeon.

Hestia looked at Bell as he passed by. The boy paused for a moment, just past the broken mug. A sudden feeling of dread overtook her; she had to stall him.

"All finished cleaning up, Goddess! If you could turn off the magic-stone lamps before leaving, that'd be great!"

"Ah...Bell!"

Hestia managed to get words out of her mouth the moment that Bell had one hand on his light-armor-filled backpack, and the door handle in the other. She knew that there was no way she could convince to him to stay here today just because she "had a bad feeling." She didn't fully understand it herself.

However, she couldn't ignore the tightness in her chest, either. She felt like the cup was trying to warn her. Hestia finally took her eyes off of it and looked up.

"A, ah—...Wha...what about your status? We haven't updated it in a few days, yeah?"

"That's...true..."

"What are you worried about? It'll only take a minute, so...please?"

Hestia tried so hard to hide her unease that a confused smile emerged on her face. Seeing this very strange look appear on his goddess, Bell let his eyebrows relax and accepted her offer.

Hestia did her best to get the cup out of her mind and quickly set to work.

"...So, um, Bell. How are things with your supporter?"

"Goddess...you've asked that at least ten times already."

"I-is that so?"

The silence was getting to her, so Hestia said the first thing that she could come up with to start a conversation, but it only got an uncomfortable smile out of Bell.

Hestia had her own reasons for wanting to know exactly what was going on during the days that Bell and Lilly went into the Dungeon together, and as a result had been asking almost nonstop since she'd allowed them to work together.

Her face went red as she sat on the small of Bell's back. Pricking her finger on a needle, she drew out the ikoru—the power in her blood—and set to work inscribing hieroglyphs into Bell's back.

"Moving on, it's only been a week, right? The Kenki must have beaten the living daylights out of you. Your Defense has increased enough to close the gap with your other abilities."

"...Ha-ha-ha-hah."

Bell's empty laugh in her ears, Hestia quickened her pace.

It had become the usual pattern. Whenever Hestia updated Bell's status, her mood got steadily worse as time went on. The cause of her foul mood was, of course, the skill behind Bell's rapid growth rate: Realis Phrase.

Hestia didn't look at all amused as she suddenly asked something that had been bugging her since she'd found out about his training sessions with Aiz.

"Bell. Sorry to bring up the past, but you and that Kenki...You didn't do anything...touchy-feely, did you? Like having your head in her lap or something like that."

Bell sputtered from his facedown position on the bed until: *Cough, cough.* As she watched, his ears turned bright red.

Damn you, Wallensomething......!! Hestia clenched her teeth.

The boy's status had made a considerable jump, for some reason. Judging by Bell's reaction to Hestia's question, she had more than enough reason to believe that they had much more contact than just his head being in her lap.

That vixen! Jealousy reared its ugly head in Hestia's heart.

"A-ah, Goddess! Do you know if my status can go up without fighting monsters in combat? Like, through training?"

Ran away, didn't you? Hestia thought, but didn't make any comment on the matter. She was a goddess, after all. She had the ability to do that much.

Her needle hand slipped.

Bell could only whimper in pain. Hestia ignored it as she answered the question.

"Yes, it'll grow. Excelia can be gained through fighting monsters or training to do so. However, playing around will do nothing for you. Remember that only hard, honest work will leave an excelia imprint that I can use to make your abilities increase."

"So what you're saying is..."

"Whether you're taking your experience seriously or not. Your focus determines the excelia that is left behind. After that, all gods have to do is find them in a status update."

This winding conversation was close to Hestia's way of explaining how to use his Skill, but she didn't come right out and say it. She thought that putting it this way would be easiest for Bell to understand.

Once Hestia finished updating Bell's status, she sat back for a moment to see what it said. Her lips started to quiver.

"Dah...! Goddess, look at the time. Sorry, I've got to get moving!"

Bell happened to look up at the clock and started to get up.

Shifting his weight to the side so that the goddess would fall lightly to the side, he jumped from the bed. Grabbing his backpack, Bell was out the door seconds later.

"B-Bell! Your status…!!"

"Sorry, tell me when I get home tonight! See you then!"

Bell looked very rushed as Hestia watched him close the door.

Alone now, Hestia lowered her outstretched arm and let out a long sigh.

She glanced up at the broken mug on the table again, before sitting up to look at the spot where Bell had been just seconds earlier.

She thought about what see had seen written on his back.

Bell Cranell

Level One

Strength: S 982   Defense: S 900   Utility: S 988

Agility: SS 1049   Magic: B 751

"Just what is 'SS' supposed to mean…"

Hestia put her right hand on her cheek, as if holding her head as she spoke under her breath.

The sun was starting to rise over the mountain range outside the eastern edge of Orario's city wall.

Aiz watched the sunrise from a square window in her room. She was just high enough to see over the wall and take in the more natural scenery beyond the city limits.

The still, reddish-orange morning glow reflected off her hair as she pulled it back behind her ears.

After fixing her saber—the only weapon she carried—to her waist, Aiz tapped on her wrists guards. Satisfied with how they fit her arm, she looked forward.

She was completely armed and ready.

The sunlight surrounded her in an orange outline, blue armor, silver breastplate, and hip guards all glinting in the morning glow.

She was the lady of the sword, the Kenki. Aiz looked every bit the warrior princess that had become her reputation.

"Hey, Aiz, ya still in there? How long ya gonna make us wait?"

"…I'm coming, now."

Responding to Bete's voice from the other side of the door, Aiz took one last look at her reflection before reaching for the handle.

Ten and two days had already passed since she ranked up to Level Six. Today was the day she had been waiting for: the expedition into the Dungeon.

A group of *Loki Familia* adventurers was planning to venture below the Lower Fortress, and the expedition was beginning.

Aiz had become too strong for "normal" trips into the Dungeon. This was her chance to venture to new depths, her only chance to see just how powerful she was.

"Aiz, let's get going! Let's see who can slay more monsters, too!"

"Such a pain…What the heck are ya doin' here, Tiona?"

"Look who's talking. The lowly dog should act like one and keep his tail between his legs!"

"I'm no dog, I'm a wolf, damn it! And whaddya mean by 'lowly'?!"

"You were flat-out rejected, remember? 'I have nothing to say to a lowly dog,' was it? Heh-heh!"

"Grrrrrrr!!"

The area outside her door had become noisy, but Aiz ignored them. A sudden, different sound caught her attention and she looked back outside.

A deep echo reached her ears. The morning bell towers had been struck.

She found the closest one outside her window to the east as the bell rang out again.

Ping. A sudden pain in my neck.

"……"

"Mr. Bell?"

I rub the spot with my hand as I look around the area.

A wide room with a thick, grassy floor and yellow walls. We're on the ninth floor, but I can't hide my anxiety.

Lilly's staring up at me, but there's no way I can make an excuse.

"Is there something bothering you, Mr. Bell?"

"...It's probably nothing."

...Is something watching me?

I just can't shake the feeling that there's an eye on me right now.

It doesn't feel like it wants to hurt me, or anything like that...I just feel this strange weight on my shoulders.

Lilly and I had decided that we'd prowl the tenth floor today, so I left early to get a head start. I think I saw a few adventurers a couple of floors up, but the Dungeon is still mostly empty.

There was that one beast-person adventurer a few rooms back— that guy was huge.

Could these eyes be his? He'd have no reason so follow us...but it's getting to the point that I can't just ignore this feeling.

"Lilly, could we swap equipment here?"

"Ah, yes, sure."

Looking flustered, Lilly quickly takes my protector and the base- lard off her back and hands them to me.

I get my light armor out of the backpack and equip everything, double-checking that every piece is strapped on tight.

I was hoping that the feeling of protection that this armor gives me would help alleviate some of this nervousness...but the weight in my neck and shoulders is still there.

It's putting pressure on my heart. My insides are screaming.

"Isn't this a little strange...?"

"A little strange?"

"There aren't enough monsters."

I finally mention another thing that had been bothering me for a while. Even Lilly looks back over her should and whispers, "Now that you mention it..."

The Dungeon has been eerily quiet ever since we arrived on the lower ninth. We've been here a while, too, the stairwell that leads to the lower tenth is just a room or two away, but we haven't encountered a single monster yet.

Well, there was a group of goblins running around, but they didn't attack us. It looked more like they were running away from something, actually.

Anxiety is sinking even deeper now; my guts are twisting into knots.

I've felt like this before, and it's bringing *that* back into my mind. Yes.

On that day, the Dungeon was this quiet, too.

I violently shake my head.

"M-Mr. Bell?"

"…Let's go. To the tenth floor."

My hand over my mouth to steady myself, I manage to get words out through my fingers.

I want to say, "Let's get out of here," but I just can't.

It's like my spirit is trying to push my body forward, away from here.

We enter the next room. It has two exits. One I remember leads to the stairwell—that's when it happens.

—*Now then, show me.*

Wha?

A voice, suddenly in my head. Not my voice—it's like something is talking to me from *inside*. I'm on full alert.

A second later…

"—Mrooooooo—"

My legs freeze.

"……"

"W-what was that…?"

Lilly is saying something. I don't hear her.

My ears are busy with something else.

That sound…it sounds too much like *that* sound. Every nerve of my body is on fire as the noises are on replay in my mind.

"…"

Like a rusted door with no grease, my neck clicks ever so slightly until I can see behind me.

The sound is coming from the room we were just in. There's something in the exit.

I'm hyperventilating. My fingers are shaking. I can't make a fist.

My throat won't budge, but in my mind I'm thinking, *It's not true.* My mental voice sounds like a kid crying.

Lilly's eyes are shaking; she sees it, too. I'm praying to something like my life depends on it.

Then…

"…Woouu!"

There it is.

"—Huh?"

"……"

I was right. Damn it.

Then again, there's no way I could forget *that* voice.

I don't know how many times I've heard it during nightmares. It's impossible to guess how many times I've heard similar howls from other monsters and flashed back to that day.

I can't count how many times I've been scared by *it.*

"Woooohoooohooo…"

Minotaur.

"W-why is there a Minotaur on the ninth floor…?"

That's what I'd like to know.

But there's something I *do* know.

I know this feeling of helplessness.

This despair that words can't describe, I know it too well.

My body has felt this uncontrollable shiver before.

It's the same.

Exactly the same as before.

"Mroooooooo!!"

The mad bull roars.

Its overwhelming power and force wash over my body; I can't hold it back. It's a sound powerful enough to break the fighting spirit of anything the Minotaur comes up against.

Lilly and I are no exception as a torrent of fear hits us full-force.

It takes one more step into the room, into the light. Its broad, silver weapon is stained with fresh blood.

"L-let's get out of here, Mr. Bell! We don't stand a chance! Quickly, while there's still time...Mr. Bell?"

My eyes are locked in place.

My legs aren't moving, either.

Fear has frozen my spine; I can't budge.

It might be my own body telling me to give up.

It reminds me of the scarecrow Gramps made when I was a kid. He put armor on it and everything...That's me, right now.

"Mr. Bell? *Mr. Bell?!*"

Scared scared scared scared scared scared.

So scared.

The monster is absolutely terrifying.

Tears are pumping into my eyes. My lungs are on the verge of jumping out of my chest. I can't close my jaw.

I don't have any words to describe the color my face is right now.

The Minotaur's aura gets heavier with each step of its hoofed feet. It's crushing the grass beneath it, getting closer and closer.

Fear itself has materialized in front of me. My body feels like it's about to explode.

"Mrooooooooo!"

The Minotaur springs forward like a cannonball.

The beast covers this distance between us with breathtaking speed.

I have to draw a weapon, but my arms won't move. I can't do anything.

It's over.

Its sword is raised high, poised to slice me between the neck and shoulder. And here it comes.

"—ah?!"

"Huh?"

My eyes suddenly see the ceiling, and a soft cry hits my ears.

Even before I realize I'm still alive, I sense Lilly's warm body make contact with my stomach.

I look down and see her head, as well as a heck of a lot of blood.

"L-Lilly...?"

I've been thrown to the ground. The beast didn't hit me; this has to be from the force of Lilly's tackle.

Thanks completely to her jumping into me from the side, I managed to get out of the path of the weapon. But in return, Lilly got hurt.

Did the sword hit her? No—but one of the rocks the Minotaur kicked up in its wake must have.

My body hits the ground at a shallow angle. Grass and chunks of the floor fly into the air behind me as I slide a good meder or two.

Lilly's head shifts, and a soft moan comes out of her mouth.

Gah...My whole body comes back to life, burning from the inside.

"!!"

Energy floods into my cowardly muscles as I climb to my feet.

I'm scared. I'm absolutely frightened. Utterly terrified.

Seeing that Minotaur right in front of me is even scarier than when it was at the other end of the room. I can't control my fear.

But the thought of Lilly dying is far more terrifying!

"MROOOOOOOO!!"

SORRY! I silently yell to the girl in my arms as I throw her to the side with all my might.

I don't wait to see where her small body lands. Instead I turn to face the beast's heaving, gigantic frame head-on.

I brace my teeth against my quivering lips. Staring down the beast as it raises its sword for another killing strike, I raise my right arm and scream at the top of my lungs:

"FIREBOLT!!"

"Mrooo?!"

A web of scarlet bolts of flame envelopes the Minotaur's body.

Overwhelmed by the sudden onslaught of flames, the Minotaur backs away, shrouded in cloud after cloud of sparks.

As far as I can see, there's little hope that my Magic can finish it off. But I have to try.

Fighting back fatigue, I fire again.

"YEEAAAAAAAAHHHHHHHHHHHHHHHH!!"

Again. Again. Again.

Blindly taking shot after shot, I put all my faith in the Magic.

My sharp bolts of flame keep finding their targets, explosions igniting on the monster's flesh. A new plume of flames erupts with each blast echo.

I didn't have this power *then*. The Firebolt is my one ray of hope—and I'm not letting up!

I just keep pulling that trigger in my mind.

"Haa-haa…!"

Once I come back to myself, all I can see is a cloud of black smoke.

All of the grass around me is burned; I can smell it. As for the Minotaur, I don't know. I can't see or hear it.

—I won?

With only the sound of the still-burning plants around me, I lower my arm.

"Mrooo…"

"—"

A sudden, unexpected sound pierces the silence and slams into my eardrums.

The smoke cloud parts without warning; a massive arm emerges.

The arm drops down before swinging up like a wrecking ball, and straight into my gut.

The living boulder hits my armor dead-on.

Shock waves tear through my body as my armor cracks.

"DAHH?!"

My line of sight spins. All the air is forced out of my lungs—what just happened? My mind is going in circles as I fly backward.

But there is one thing I do know: Aiz saved me.

Since my body flew back immediately, I don't absorb the full force of the blow.

Of course, that doesn't mean I felt nothing. If I'd taken that hit flat-footed, there's no doubt in my mind my stomach would have exploded. That grim thought in my mind, I fly helplessly backward and into the dungeon wall.

"—?! ...ah, gah?!"

The wall cracks on impact. A new wave of pain floods in from my back as I realize something very disheartening: I'm wedged into the wall.

I can't speak. There's a loud crack near my head and I fall bottom-first onto the floor, along with a small avalanche of rubble.

My armor is, in a word, broken. Totaled.

The back plate must have shattered; it's lying in pieces beside me. With the support piece gone, any part that was still intact fell off my body the moment my butt touched the ground.

How many times is this thing going to send me flying?!

Reduced to only my damaged and torn inner shirt, I climb to my feet on trembling legs.

"Hnnnnfff...!"

"......!"

Its face is scrunched. It looks angry.

But not hurt.

I hit it with more Firebolts than I can remember, but there it is, the picture of health. I can't even see a wound on its body.

Sure, burn marks are scattered all over it, but there's nothing even close to life-threatening.

I'm too weak.

With a quick glare at my stunned face, the Minotaur throws back its head and howls toward the ceiling.

"MROOOOOOOOOOOOAAAAAHH!!"

So this is an *adventure*.

The first one for the adventurer, Bell Cranell.

—It's hopeless. I can't win.

I can only see despair as I look at the ferocious beast in front of me.

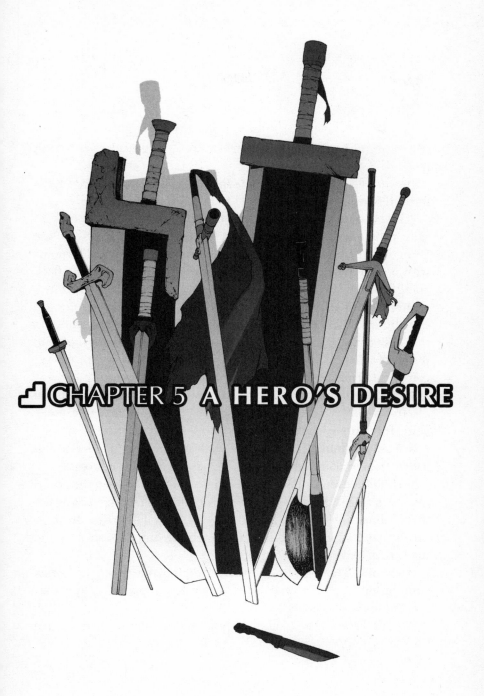

CHAPTER 5 A HERO'S DESIRE

© Suzuhito Yasuda

It's common knowledge that the Dungeon gets wider with each floor.

The fifth floor is about the same size as Central Park. However, the fortieth floor is rumored to rival Orario itself in size and scale.

While there are some floors that don't follow this pattern exactly, most people have accepted the idea that the deeper you go into the Dungeon, the broader the floors become. The hallways and rooms within each floor also increase dramatically in size with each floor going down.

This creates an interesting problem for battle parties going on expeditions. These parties are typically large groups of adventurers that have come together to go as deep into the Dungeon as they can. It's no problem to move together on the lower floors, but things get complicated on the narrower upper floors of the Dungeon.

A full expedition party on the first few floors is the very definition of a traffic jam. All the cargo crates, along with lines of people, make going forward nearly impossible.

Not only do monsters have to be dealt with in a smaller space, but it also blocks the movements of other adventurers in the area.

Therefore, several rules have been implemented to keep the peace. One such rule is that expeditions will go into the Dungeon in two or three groups and meet up at a predetermined point farther down.

Loki Familia was no different. They broke into two groups and made their way into the Dungeon.

"Hey, hey, Tione. Why are there people from another *Familia* coming with us? We don't need that many supporters, and they don't look the part at all…"

"Stupid Tiona. Have you already forgotten why we had to turn back last time?"

"?"

"They are smiths, Tiona."

"Ah!"

Fynn Dimuna, the prum field general of *Loki Familia*, led a group of top-class adventurers through the winding halls of the lower-seventh floor.

Their party consisted of fifteen people, Tiona, Tione, and the elf Reveria among them.

"Our weapons failed us before we ran out of strength during our previous Expedition. The general was kind enough to find an answer."

"As long as we have smiths that know the Forge skill with us, we'll always have sharp blades! Nice one, Fynn!"

"It was unreasonable to bring another cargo box just for spares. Turns out Loki and the Goddess Hephaistos are good friends, and we couldn't have set this up without her."

"Come to think of it, isn't it strange that we don't have smiths with a Forge in our own *Familia*. It would be nice to have one, don't you think?"

This was how *Loki Familia*'s top adventurers were before reaching the lower levels…The supporters took care of the monsters en route, and the strongest adventurers could only kill time until the group made it farther down.

They might have seemed carefree on the surface as they waited for their turn at the front of the caravan, but a large amount of vigor dwelled within each of them.

"Aiz! Hey, Aiz! You hear that? Some of *Hephaistos Familia*'s High Smiths are coming with us!"

"Yes…I heard. That's great."

"You bet it is! Now we can go crazy on the lower levels! This is going to be so much fun!"

"Just to let you know, even *Hephaistos Familia*'s High Smiths can't fix a shattered blade. Don't forget."

Tiona had run up to Aiz and wrapped her arms around the shoulder of the quietly walking Aiz as she spoke. Aiz lightly smiled when she turned to face the young Amazon.

A big grin bloomed on Tiona's face upon seeing Aiz's reaction.

The vast majority of Amazons were not like her. Tiona would have been much more at home if she were born into another race. But her warmth and energy had succeeded in melting the wall of ice that was Aiz Wallenstein.

Tiona's younger sister Tione was quick to warn her sister, but still sounded playful. Despite the three girls being absolute powerhouses in combat, they could still enjoy teasing each other as friends.

"All right. As long as these guys are from *Hephaistos Familia*, they ain't gonna get in our way, even if they screw up. That's a relief."

"It was just a matter of time. Bete's macho complex is at it again."

Still clinging to Aiz's shoulder, Tiona turned to look at her ally, a twitch in her eye.

"Got a problem?" Bete responded, glaring back at the girl and baring his fangs.

"Bete, why do you always say things like that? Does it feel that good to look down on others? Honestly, I can't stand that about you."

"Don't get the wrong idea. It'd be embarrassin' to get all high 'n' mighty by comparin' myself to small fry like that! Just bein' realistic, here!"

Bete jerked his head back toward the High Smiths and said, "Was payin' 'em a compliment."

"You must learn the power of your words. The way you said that makes me believe you want us to get the wrong idea."

"Oh-ho-ho! Shut it! I've had it with you elves and yer teachings! Don't go butting inta other's conversations either, Reveria!"

The sharp, ash-gray fur covering Bete's head and shoulders ruffled as he snarled back at the elf.

The lips around his jagged teeth softened as his cheeks relaxed.

"Who are ya ta talk, anyway? All ya high 'n' mighty elves are thinkin' the same thing. Can ya tell me straight that ya don't get pissed when ya see some weaklin' tryin' ta run with the big boys?"

"Tione just stole everything from meeeee!!"

"Stop the strange accusations, will you…"

"While it would be a lie to say that I have never once felt pity for them, do not compare my compassion with your contempt."

"Ya know what? Just by takin' pity on wimps makes the high 'n' mighty elves seem snooty—ya get me?"

Fynn let out a long, heavy sigh as Bete and Reveria continued their argument.

He knew that Bete was making a point about how elves in general interacted with other races, and not making a personal attack on Reveria. Then again, werewolf animal people were not known for their acceptance of others, either, particularly Bete.

Arguments like this were nothing new between these two; in fact, it was almost normal. Reveria often started them when Bete said something she couldn't agree with.

Fynn and the rest of the group knew this as well, so no one tried to stop them. Even Aiz watched quietly a few paces behind them.

"I just *despise* weak trash. Actin' all tough when they can't do jack shit! Makes me sick just thinkin' 'bout it!"

"All I hear is overconfidence from someone who once walked in their shoes."

"She's right, Bete, wasn't that long ago you were weak."

"Know your place, that's all I'm sayin'."

Tiona still hanging off her shoulders, Aiz quietly repeated "your place" under her breath.

She had some thoughts on that.

For her, it wasn't pity, contempt, or disgust, but a clear question.

How did a boy who hated his place so much manage to rise so high since that time? What drove him?

Aiz couldn't remember much about the first time she met him, just his ruby-red eyes about to burst into tears.

That's when it happened.

Without warning, Aiz snapped to attention.

"…Maybe four?"

"What's that, those rumored somethin' or others?"

One by one, other members of the group found the source of a sound coming their way. Tiona shifted her weight to Aiz's other shoulder for a closer look, as Bete's wolf ears zeroed in on the oncoming intersection.

Echoes of hurried footsteps barreled around the right corner of the four-way crossing. Judging from the sound, they were panicked steps.

Supporters quickly jumped in front of their leader as shields against an ambush, but Fynn raised an arm and waved them off. He told them they didn't have to move from their posts.

At last, the party of adventurers came around the corner.

"They seem to be in a rush. Should we ask why?"

"That's out of the question. We can't interfere with another party within the Dungeon."

"Hey, you guys! Where's the fire?"

Ignoring her sister's warning, Tiona called out to the approaching battle party.

All four of the adventurers were running while looking over their shoulders, as if they were being chased. Tiona's voice made them all stop on a dime and jump backward in surprise.

"W-what the heck are...? Huh? An Amazon?!"

"Tiona Hyrute?!"

"Wait—*Loki Familia*?! An expedition?!"

All of them stopped, shaking in surprise and completely star-struck at the sight of the top-class adventurers before them.

Tiona flinched as one of them started screaming bloody murder, but Bete didn't think anything of it and approached them.

"Right, quiet now. We're askin' the questions, you're answerin'. What the hell were you doin'? Run into a horde of killer ants or somethin'? Abandon a supporter or two t'get away?"

"How dare you accuse...?!"

"Oi, out with it."

"...Compared to *that*, I'd take one hundred killer ants any day!"

The man spoke like the words were falling out of his mouth. Bete raised his shoulders in suspicion.

Looking at all of them in succession, Bete lowered his eyebrows as if asking for more information. The adventurers exchanged glances at one another before a human, most likely their leader, stepped forward.

"...There was a Minotaur."

"...Yeah?"

"A Minotaur, I tell you! It's walking around the upper levels!"

Seeing the lack of color in the man's face, Bete looked back over his shoulder at the rest of his own party.

Fynn and the others hadn't joined in the conversation, but heard everything. Each wore a sour expression.

Even though no one was looking at her, Aiz's right hand started to shake.

"You don't think...Could it be one of the ones that got away from us?"

"Not possible. We got every single one, didn't we?"

"It would be very strange if it was one of ours, even if we did over-look it. A month has passed since that expedition. If a Minotaur were lurking up here, there would have been an appalling amount of casualties among the lower ranks of adventurers. That kind of infor-mation has yet to reach my ears."

"...My apologies. But would you mind explaining what you saw in detail?"

"Ah...sure."

Fynn approached the other party's leader and asked him face-to-face. The leader began talking about what happened.

He said that they were on a usual route when they saw two fig-ures at the end of a long hallway: a Minotaur and a white-haired boy.

The boy's screams and the Minotaur's howls echoed through the hall and scared them half to death. They had been running full-out ever since.

The leader then added that the Minotaur was equipped with a cleaver.

"A cleaver—?"

"Not a landform?"

"Y-yes...There's no doubt."

"...Had you heard anything about a Minotaur before seeing it today?"

"Hell, no! You think we'd come down here if we did?"

"General...?"

"Yeah...this sounds really fishy."

While the members of *Loki Familia* were able to confirm it was not one that they were responsible for, it only raised more questions about this new Minotaur.

Fynn, whose intuition was usually spot-on, suggested that this was a prank by some god with a grudge.

At the very least, a god had to be involved in this incident. There was no other logical explanation.

The rest of the expedition party had caught up to the conversation and came to a halt.

"Where did you see the Minotaur?"

Amid the mass of humanity, one blond head moved forward.

Her voice was soft as she walked just within earshot of the party of four.

"Huh?"

"On which floor did you see an adventurer fighting a Minotaur?"

"The n-ninth...if they haven't moved..."

The instant she heard the number, Aiz shot off into the Dungeon.

"AIZ?!"

"What the heck are you doing?!"

"Hey you guys, we're on an expedition here?!"

"......Fynn?"

"Yes, I know...The party will advance! Take the shortest possible route to the lower eighteenth! Raul, you're in charge!"

"S-Sir?"

"'In charge'...Which means you plan to investigate personally?"

"Just until I get back. I want to see this through. Reveria, don't tell me you're planning to stay with the expedition?"

"...If your feelings are telling you to go, Fynn, I shall accompany you whether you like it or not."

"Ha-ha-ha!"

Members of *Loki Familia* and *Hephaistos Familia* stood in stunned silence as a small group of top-tier adventurers took off into the Dungeon.

The small group was on a new quest—to find answers on the lower ninth.

Gramps's face.

I don't want to see my grandfather's face.

With my parents gone, he was the one who raised me.

He'd always get this funny look in his eye and say things like, "Sure would like to save some cute girls and score!" or "Serving the ladies is the definition of romance!" or "Nothing wrong with playing the game!" and even "Just don't go cheating, you hear?" He said some other things that I didn't understand, too, but he was always upbeat and cheerful.

He often told me stories about heroes that were so vivid, it was like I was actually in the party with them.

It was a long time after he died that I found out that he drew all of the pictures in the book he gave me for my birthday all those years ago.

—They're really something else!

—Any one of them can stand up to an enemy even stronger than themselves.

—Not possible for a geezer like me.

While claiming he was nothing compared to them, he always did so with a big smile on his face.

But it was a lie to say he didn't do anything heroic.

Gramps was legendary.

When I was a kid and a goblin was about to kill me, he charged that monster like a bolt of lightning, armed with nothing but a garden hoe.

He always wore loose clothing, but at that moment I realized how big his muscles were, how powerful he was. He shone like a warrior that day.

Even when another two goblins showed up, Gramps stood his ground and shielded me. I still remember his arms, thick as tree trucks as he wielded his "weapon."

And then he embraced me. I'd never felt safer than when I could feel his big hands on my back.

Now that I think about it…

The first hero I idolized was my grandfather.

If you're in danger, run.

If you're scared, get away.

If you're about to die, call for help.

If a woman is angry, apologize immediately.

It's not embarrassing to get made fun of or picked on.

The most embarrassing thing is not being able to make up your mind and take action.

Gramps was always saying that.

Even after he disappeared from my life, his teachings are still with me. Gramps was the one who gave me my drive.

His words led me to Orario in the first place.

But I don't want him to see me like this. I can't bear to see his face.

"MROOOOOOOOOOOOOOOOOOOOOOOOOOOOOOOOOOO!!"

Gramps.

Right now, I can't move.

"…N…ah."

I lift my head up only to see a stream of saliva dripping out of the Minotaur's mouth.

The monster is still a ways away from me, but it's howling and brandishing its sword over and over, as though gloating.

I can see the beast's whole body, its fur like heavy armor. Even

after all those Firebolt impacts, there are no deep wounds anywhere
on its massive frame.

The realization that my Magic won't work makes me feel absolutely powerless, my body weak and empty.

I can't win. I have no idea how many times those words have
echoed through my head.

My arms and legs won't move.

I get to my feet, but my knees are shaking. They could buckle at
any moment.

"Hnnfff…!!"

"……?!"

I feel a chill in my spine as the monster's eyes lock onto me again.

The cold fear that had enveloped me up to this point is replaced by
despair, as all the muscles in my body go slack.

My mind is going full-speed, but my instincts tell me the end is near.

I'll be pulverized by the next hit.

Both Lilly and I are as good as dead.

I have to move…!

My fingers start to twitch.

"MROOOOOOO!"

—I'm too close to the wall!

The second I see the Minotaur make a move for me, I get my ass
moving.

That thing is so big that if my back is against the wall, I won't be
able to dodge or escape.

First priority: get into the open field. Running away from Lilly, I
make a break for the middle of the room.

The Minotaur's eyes follow my every move. It sees where I'm going
and makes a sharp turn, its feet sending dirt flying as it charges in
from my right side.

It's coming up fast!

I can see it growing huge in my shaking eyes.

"MROOONN!!"

"—Grk!!"

It kicks the ground and goes airborne.

I have no choice but to do the same, to have any chance at avoiding the oncoming cleaver.

I just clear the blade, my body snaking out of the way of the cutting edge as I dive forward.

The shock wave from the blade's impact behind me makes me lose my balance the second my hands hit the ground, shivers running up my spine. But I manage to tuck my chin into my chest and roll a few times before jumping up to my feet.

Spin around, back step.

The ground beneath my feet is cracked, the break starting back at the blood-soaked cleaver, still in the monster's grasp. The beast glares at me as I put more space between us as fast as I can.

"MROOOOAAAAAAH!!"

But the moment it plants its massive hoof on the ground, the Minotaur instantly reduces the distance to zero.

My eyes are wide in surprise as it holds the cleaver in both hands, preparing for a full swing.

I feel my face turn a dark red.

Hearing the sound of wind being torn asunder, I fall to my knees and duck with all my might. I feel the power of the beast's swing as the edge of the monstrous sword passes just above my head.

I feel like my shadow just got sliced in half—that's how close it came to taking my head clean off my shoulders. It cut some of the hair off the back of my head.

"MROOOAH!!"

"Hnn?!"

Amid a small flurry of white human hair, my hair, the Minotaur swings the blade down on my crouching body. I roll forward as if my body were shot out of a cannon. *BANG!*

That's where the onslaught starts.

The Minotaur swings down again and again, the blood-splattered sliver blade aimed right at my neck. No matter which direction I go, I can't get out of the blade's reach. Soon, punches and kicks graze my body. I can't see where they're coming from, but if I stop rolling, it's all over!

Each heartbeat, each breath burns in my chest.

The realization that one wrong move means certain death clamps down on my brain like a vice.

The alarm bells in my head keep going.

My ears are going to shatter.

"?!…Guh?!"

By the time I notice, my body is a wreck. But what did I expect would happen after rolling on the floor that much, just barely avoiding killing blow after killing blow from the Minotaur's rampage?

There's no room for error, and how could there be? I'm so covered in cuts and bruises that I've practically got one foot in the grave already.

If these attacks keep coming…

Vague images of the future in my head now feel strange.

I dodged the final blow by a hair, again.

It's just a matter of time. Even if I manage to dodge another, I can't avoid death.

Run away.

Get out of here, there's no choice!

If I don't escape, no one can save me!

"Mister…Bell……"

My eyes snap to the sound. A small mound of earth flinches away.

It's Lilly. Her whole body is unsteady, like she could fall at any moment. She's looking at me, her eyes cloudy. She's still bleeding, a red streak running down her cheek.

I scream with everything I have left in my lungs:

"Lilly, get out of here!"

My voice almost shrieks as a new shiver passes through her body.

Jumping back to avoid the cleaver yet again, I yell at her over and over to run.

But she's not moving. She's just standing there looking at me, about to cry.

Gah...This is so frustrating!

"Run...Get the hell out of here!"

She shakes her head no, tears streaming out of her eyes. Is she not thinking clearly? She's acting like a spoiled child who's not getting her way.

WHY?!

As long as you're here, I can't run!

Once you get away, I can escape!

Don't you understand? Why don't you get it? I'm begging you, wake up!!

"GET GOING!! NOOOW!!!"

Anger fills my voice as I scream at her again.

Tears pouring down her bloody face, she turns her back to me.

Tup, tup, tup. She takes off and disappears from the room.

Yes! Now I can make my escape!

Finally, I can get out of here!

I can leave...

Like hell I can...?!

If I'm gone, what's to stop this bastard from chasing her down?

If this mad cow goes after her, Lilly will...Lilly's going to...

"...DAMN IT!!"

I jam my right hand into my protector and pull out the baselard.

Coming up from one last roll and throwing my leg into the dirt, I face the beast head-on.

I don't know if I want to be angry or if I want to cry. My mind is already a wreck from everything that's happened, I can't think straight.

I engage the Minotaur in combat out of desperation.

"MROOOOAAAAAAAHHH!!"

"?!"

I quickly get out of the way of a sudden punch and bring the baselard down on its wrist.

Feeling the backlash down my right arm, I jump back to dodge a slash from the cleaver. There's no way the baselard could block that amount of sheer force.

I land and brace for the next attack.

My wide-eyed gaze locks with the beast's sharp glare.

"ROAAA, WAOO, OOOOH!!"

"Gah!"

I continue to dodge blow after blow, dancing with death without any armor at all. The cleaver slams into the ground over and over, each time showering me and my wounds with dirt and rubble.

The Minotaur's breath is heavy and ragged. Is it getting frustrated because it can't hit me?

Meanwhile, my breathing is even, almost calm. Sure, I'm sweating like there's no tomorrow. I feel like I could drink a lake right now.

Waves of power blast out of each of the Minotaur's attacks again and again, but flow harmlessly out over the prairie. Every sound in the Dungeon right now is coming from this battle alone.

Two shadows dueling in a vast, grass-covered room, under one light on the ceiling far above.

"FOO...WWOOOOOOHH!!"

I can feel the beast's rage in its howls.

Like it's yelling, "Stand still!"

Only after working up the courage to face it with only the baselard for defense do I see that my Agility is of a level with the beast's.

But I can't press forward.

Each time an attack whizzes by my head, I get cold feet and take a step back. I'm still too scared.

Don't advance.

Focus on the retreat.

Dodge, dodge, dodge. Buy as much time as possible.

Just as long as I can live to see another second, that's good enough...!

Right...?!

"Ha-ahh!"

I breathe hard as I duck under yet another powerful sideswipe.

I've lost count of how many times I've seen death pass by my face. I've got shallow cuts all over my cheeks from near misses. My heart feels like it's being strangled by the power of the beast's aura.

I may be trembling, but I'm still here, still running.

Managing to jump out of the way of a downward slash of the cleaver, I see a hole in the Minotaur's attack pattern. With its body folded down and the sword out in front, it can't attack to the side without me seeing it coming. A safe spot!

Just as I jump into the open area, the Minotaur's eyes narrow.

"___"

Fuhh-fuhh. Its heavy breaths filling my ears, the Minotaur takes its eyes off the massive sword and whips its neck around to face me.

"—Dah?!"

It had one option from that position I didn't think of—a head butt.

And on top of its head and coming right at me, a horn!

The tip of its thick, curved horn is aimed right at my chest!

"Yeeh?!"

Even though I knew it was about as useful as tissue paper, I brace my protector in front of the oncoming spearhead. The horn penetrates the protector like a knife through butter.

Thanks to the angle of the attack, I escape another killing blow. By some miracle, even my arm is in one piece, with just a shallow gash across the front of my left arm.

However…

The horn is stuck inside the protector.

The protector is still strapped to my arm. My feet leave the ground as the Minotaur stands up, with me hanging on.

"Gehe?!"

"OOOooWOOOO!!"

It flicks its neck, swinging me around like a rag doll.

It flips the other direction, and my body goes with it.

Every joint pops; I'm in shock. I have no idea where the ground is—all I know is that I'm two meders above it.

I can't see anything! Going too fast!

The sudden whips are getting more intense, knocking the wind out of me.

My left shoulder is at its limit, popping and pulling painfully.

Two, three more crazy swings from the beast and the protector breaks, just a second before my shoulder joint would have given out.

The protector was already broken, but now it cracks down the middle from the penetration point.

At that exact second, the Minotaur flings its head upward. My arm is free; there's nothing to stop me from flying straight up.

"UUHH—WAAAAAAAAAAAAAAAAAAAAAAA!!"

I come within touching distance of the ten-meder-high ceiling of the lower-ninth floor before feeling gravity take hold of my body.

Tracing a mountain in the Dungeon, I start my descent.

Unable to brace my body for impact, the ceiling falls away from me—fast.

"GeHAAHH!"

I land flat on my back.

A scream of pain shoots through my spine and out to every nerve in my body. Stars are flashing in my eyes.

I can feel my arms and legs convulsing, again and again.

If it weren't for my Defense, I'd already be dead...?!

"Aa...ah?!"

My eyes won't stop blinking.

The wave of pain forces sounds out of my mouth. I scrunch up my forehead and force my eyes closed.

But I can feel the Minotaur, the impact of its footsteps coming through the ground.

This is bad, but there's nothing I can do anymore. I can't move; I can only make the strange sounds coming out of my throat.

Not being able to move brings back the terror I'd been holding down by sheer force of will. The fear is back with a vengeance.

Click, click—my teeth start chattering. Tears begin to flow out of my eyes.

Scared.

I've never been so scared.

I'm in pain. Everything hurts. I'm overwhelmed.

But above all that...

I'm absolutely terrified.

Too scared to stand.

"Uuuh…!"

The vibrations of the oncoming footsteps make my hair stand on end. It's coming closer, slowly.

I'll be slaughtered. Panic is taking the feeling out of my arms and legs.

The fear is taking me, breaking me. But if I give in, will that make what's about to happen painless?

I open my eyes to see the bright lights overhead. Each of their light beams silently reflect off my tears.

—It's over.

The terror within me pushes every shred of hope I had left out of my body in one long sigh.

"…?"

The vibrations stop.

The execution block that I can't escape from has become eerily quiet.

In the place of the vibrations, a breeze.

How strange. What happened? I'm caught between terror and curiosity. What's going on?

I relax my face and try to move.

My body is still quivering, but I manage to raise my head off the ground.

That's when…

"—"

…I see her.

"…"

Long, flowing blond hair. Blue armor. Thin, sliver saber.

Just like she had a day before, the female knight has her back to me.

Time stands still.

"Uhh…uwooo…?!"

The Minotaur is afraid.

Its eyes locked on the silent warrior, it takes several shaky steps backward.

I feel wind.

And she's at the center, her presence filling the room and forcing complete stillness.

Her aura has taken over.

—The Kenki. Aiz Wallenstein.

"Found her! Hey, Aiz!!"

"Heh, ya drag me all the way down here for somethin' this boring? Pathetic!"

More vibrations of footprints through the ground, even new voices in my ears, but I can't take my eyes off her back.

Her eye and the tip of her nose.

Aiz is shielding me from the Minotaur, facing it down.

My head is all mixed up. What's going on?

What's going to happen?

My torso comes off the ground as if pulled up by invisible ropes. I don't even notice, my attention completely on the girl in front of me.

"...Are you okay?"

—Am I okay?

Just like the first time.

Her standing in front of me, looking back over her shoulder, her thin face saying those words.

Everything in my body shudders as if struck by lightning.

"...You did well."

I did...well?

Unlike the last time.

Words of sympathy, encouragement.

Ba-bash! My heart thrashes.

"I'll save you now."

Save...me?

My heart pounds away in my chest.

Everything else in my line of sight suddenly snaps back into color.

Everything is white hot.

Save?

Being saved?

Again?

By her?

Just like before?

Like a pattern?

Who?

—Me.

"...?!"

A fire lights within me.

That spark grows into an inferno that purges all other emotions from my mind.

The fear disappears as the blaze roars through.

A new strength, one I've never known, uses the flame to fill my body with power.

Stand.

Stand up!

STAND UP NOW!!

How long are you going to just lay there?!

How many times are you just going to let her save you?!

I've seen this once before!

I can't stand being saved by her yet again! I won't allow it!!

"_____?!"

Body, move forward!

If you've got enough time to be afraid, make up your mind!

She's your idol! Do you want her to see you like this *again*?

She's the one you want to impress—don't show her anything more embarrassing than you already have. What good will that do?

I can't stand it, I won't stand it, I refuse to put up with it!

If I can't impress her now, when can I?!

If now isn't a good time to look her in the eyes, when is a good time?!

If I can't stand up on my feet now, when will I?

If I can't reach a new height now, *when the hell will I*?!

My legs kick off the ground.

I'm up and moving again.

"?!"

"...can't..."

I grab hold of her hand.

It feels so thin and delicate that I might break it if I squeeze too hard. I gently pull her around behind me.

I'm going forward; it's my choice.

"I can't be saved by Aiz Wallenstein yet again!"

I yell from the pit of my gut as I grab my knife.

The Minotaur sees me step forward. Its eyes pop open for a moment before it greats me with vicious laughter.

As if granting my wish, the beast points the tip of the cleaver in my direction.

"I challenge you...!"

It's time for an adventure.

For the part of me that has to know.

Today, for the first time, I find out what's on the other side of the wall.

The boy charged.

Aiz, stunned, watched as the little rabbit rushed headlong toward the monstrous bull.

"Well, it's goin' against the rules ta steal someone else's kill. Looks like ya got rejected, Aiz."

"......"

Bete's carefree, almost joking voice came up from behind the now alone Aiz.

He continued by saying that the kid was in the right, being an adventurer.

Bete and Tiona were the first to enter the room behind Aiz, follow closely by Tione and finally Reveria and Fynn.

They all arrived just in time to see Bell engage the Minotaur in combat.

Bete's eyes followed the boy's movements as Bell cleanly dodged the monster's first strike. "Ohh!" he said in surprise, his mouth an open circle. "Ahh?" He noticed something peculiar.

"White head there...isn't that tomato boy? Keh! Ha-ha-ha-ha! Poor kid! Looks like Minotaurs have a thing for 'im!"

"You mean the one Aiz saved at the last moment?"

"That's him, all right! Can you see the hearts in the 'Taur's eyes? It's love for White Head that made the beastie run all the way up here just to be with him!"

"Stop messing around, Bete."

Bete just shrugged at Tione's warning.

A smirk appeared on his wolfish muzzle as the wolf man looked back at the battle.

"Fine, fine. But I ain't gonna go rescue the kid. White Head got his ass saved just like this not too long ago, and ran off like the weakling he is then, too."

"Are you sure about this? He's Level One, right? The Minotaur will gut him for sure!"

"Tomato boy made his decision. It's not our place. Ain't that right, Tione?"

"Would you leave me out of this?"

Bete saw a tick of annoyance on Tione's face, but he couldn't care less. So he turned his focus back to the battle, a smile still on his face.

The three adventurers stood in a small circle, but Tiona couldn't sit still. She wanted to help the boy, not see him die.

"Either way, we can't just ignore that monster! We clean it up before or after the boy dies, that's it! I for one am going to help!"

"Leave 'im. The kid's bein' a man. Any idea how painful it'd be to be saved again now after bein' humiliated before? If it were me, death would be better than goin' through that again."

"I don't care about your aesthetics, Bete!"

The three of them forgot where they were for a moment, laughing at themselves. But under their chuckles, there was a voice that struggled to be heard.

A small shadow at their side, barely able to stand.

"...Please, honorable adventurers. Mr. Bell...please save Mr. Bell..."

"L-little prum..."

"Hey, hands off! I said, OFF!"

The completely unchanged, natural Lilly fell forward, grabbing onto Bete's clothes to keep herself from falling.

"Lilly will repay. Lilly will do anything, absolutely anything... Please save Mr. Bell...please...!"

"W-what did I just say..."

As the young prum got more and more desperate, Bete looked down at her with his wolf ears pinned back. But after seeing the girl's face, only then did his expression soften.

Reveria glided up behind Lilly and crouched down behind her, putting her right hand in front of the prum's eyes. She then wrapped her left arm around the girl's stomach and drew her into an embrace.

"Do not strain yourself. Wounds may close, but spilt blood has yet to replenish."

As soon as Reveria finished her spell, a jade light erupted from her right hand, illuminating Lilly's eyes. Just as the high elf had just said, Lilly's wounds came together; the stream of blood running down her face went dry.

It was no coincidence that *Loki Familia*'s adventurers appeared in this room—it was all thanks to Lilly.

Even though she should have escaped after leaving Bell behind, she kept running circles around the lower-ninth floor, injuries and all, desperately looking for help. That's when she found Aiz.

Endless pleading from the supporter to help her friend led *Loki Familia* to this room.

"Please save...please...save......"

"...Tsk."

Bete had reached his limit. He snapped his tongue as he looked down at the incoherent girl.

He scratched the back of his head, ash-colored fur rippling. Clearing his throat, Bete took a step toward Aiz and the battle farther beyond.

"Are you going?"

"Don't go gettin' the wrong idea, I hate savin' trash. But I just can't stand bein' begged to save somebody weaker than me from torment. That's worse."

Bete didn't even look at Reveria as he gave her a blunt answer.

"Outta the way, Aiz. It's mine!"

"......"

"Hey, what'cha starin'...at..."

Bete had advanced as far as Aiz's position when he came to a sudden halt.

Just as usual, Aiz's face was devoid of emotion—with the exception of her golden eyes. They were wide open in surprise.

She was watching the scene unfold with the utmost intensity.

"...Huh?"

Bete looked that way.

And his jaw dropped.

The Minotaur, swinging a massive cleaver, and a boy wielding a knife.

Neither was giving ground as their blades clashed again and again.

"......Wha...?"

Their battle filled the room with layer upon layer of metallic echoes.

But not all were the same; some of the vibrations carried a force that felt strong enough to destroy anything. Others felt so fast that they could slice through any material.

Bete's ears braced for impact over and over as the psychotic melody spread throughout the Dungeon.

His eyes followed the sliver flashes of the cleaver and the violet streaks of the knife. Just when it looked as though a burst of silver was going to connect, a violet arc intercepted its path, adding yet another clashing echo.

Bell and the Minotaur locked eyes as they continued to trade attack and defense. Neither was backing down.

"Eh...huh, wha...?"

"...Who is Level One?"

The battle had caught Tiona's and the others' attention.

It was obvious to everyone present that the Minotaur had an advantage, just from its size alone. However, all of them could see that it wasn't a one-sided battle, not by a long shot.

It was a duel, both sides evenly matched in a fight to the death.

A sudden high note in the echo melody pierced their ears.

Tiona's group took their eyes off the battle as Bell blocked the cleaver with his knife yet again and looked in Bete's direction. All of them were looking for answers.

Bete didn't know how to respond.

"If my memory is correct…"

A calm voice cut through the chaos.

Bete's shoulders dropped, a look of shock that even he didn't comprehend on his face, as he turned around to face the speaker.

Their leader, Fynn Dimuna, took small, calculated steps as he quietly approached. He stopped just behind Bete before continuing.

"Isn't this the boy who, one month ago, you considered to be 'the newest of the newbies,' Bete?"

"……"

A burst of sparks lit up their faces.

The instant the bright red light faded, a shock wave from the combatants' blades passed between them, ruffling hair, fur, and clothes on its way by.

Fynn didn't budge, his blue gaze looking up at Bete, who was squinting to protect his own eyes.

The boy was a newbie, there was no doubt.

He knew nothing of combat and was getting run around in circles by a Minotaur. One look had told Bete all he needed to know.

He was a pathetic, laughable excuse for an adventurer.

This boy.

What the hell happened?!

He had become so much more.

The person who was engaging this Minotaur in a fight to the death was not the weak trash that he despised.

The boy had visible potential, a genuine rookie.

Just one month. That's all it took.

Even adventurers who started off with talent and combat experience couldn't improve so much that their very aura changed in a span of thirty days. By and large, adventurers improved at a snail's pace.

He'd made an unbelievable jump from rock bottom to where he is now.

Bete stood there in awe.

This ain't freakin' possible! Lost in thought, confusion took over as Bete once again counted the days it took for Bell's transformation.

No matter how hard he tried, Bete couldn't find any possible explanation. That realization sent shivers down his spine.

"..."

Standing right next to him, Aiz was also fixed on Bell.

While there was a glint of surprise in her golden eyes, her expression had shifted to one of interest.

"UWAAAAAOOOOOOOOOOOOOOO!!"

"HAAAAAAAAAAAAAAAAAA!!"

The combatants' voices joined the chorus of metal clashes.

The human and the Minotaur collided again and again in a battle of strength against speed.

The Amazon sisters had joined Bete and Aiz to get a front-row seat for the battle. Reveria wasn't far behind, with Lilly resting in her arms.

They stood in a line, their jaws slack as they watched the ebb and flow of every attack with unblinking eyes.

"..."

The elite adventurers of *Loki Familia* watched the duel to the death from the sidelines.

By their standards, this was a very crude battle.

A low-level skirmish that wasn't even worth their time.

However, there was something about it that captivated them. At the very least, they had to know the outcome.

Some of them watched in amazement, some of them followed movements with sharp, focused eyes, still others looked on in calm silence.

Constant explosions of sparks surrounded the battle.

Whistles of air-splitting strikes rang out.

All the light in the already dim room seemed to focus on them alone, their duel in a spotlight.

It was like a page out of folklore.

A man facing down a fearsome beast in a desperate battle to the death.

Tiona squinted her eyes.

"Argonaut..."

That was one of the legends.

It was the story of a boy who dreamed of becoming a hero. He journeyed deep into a labyrinth to save his queen after she had been kidnapped by a bull-monster.

At times, he was fooled by others.

The king even manipulated him on multiple occasions.

His desire to help others sent him in many different directions along the way. But it was meant to be a humorous tale.

The boy made many friends, borrowing their knowledge.

He received weapons from fairies.

Every one of his endeavors somehow led to his rescuing of the queen, making his name known throughout the land. The kind, funny, and yet heroic Argonaut.

"I've always liked...that story..."

Tiona clasped her hands in front of her chest, her eyes glistening as if she had discovered a vast treasure as the battle unfolded in front of her.

Nostalgia swept over her as she smiled, memories of the story flooding her mind.

Like ripples through water, each of her comrades made the connection to that legendary tale, the sounds of battle still filling their ears.

The battle still raged on before them, flashes of white and red continuously plowing into each other.

The elite adventurers looked on as a fairy tale came to life right before their eyes.

My body is light.

My mind is clear.

My soul is on fire.

A massive sword passes my face, and I charge forward.

I challenge the monster's howls with roars of my own, and press forward.

My entire body is focused, looking for a chance to seize victory, pressing forward.

The only thing that matters is the enemy in front of me.

Well, this is a first.

This isn't some pathetic fantasy.

I'm not caught up in my own ego.

I'm not daydreaming; this isn't some unattainable wish.

I want to be a hero.

A hero who can take this thing down.

This is the first time I've wished from my heart that I wasn't some weak kid, but someone who is a heroic man.

I—

I want to be…a hero.

"……!"

Clatter.

A chair fell over as Freya jumped to her feet.

Bell and the Minotaur were in the middle of their battle.

A look of shock overtook Freya's face as she watched the battle through a window floating in the middle of her room.

"……Is this really happening?"

The Divine Mirror was one of the only Arcanum—the godly powers—that was allowed on Gekai.

Originally, it was used to allow gods and goddesses to watch the children's activities. It was a tool that opened a one-way window to any location in the world. Since its main purpose was entertainment, the Divine Mirror was exempt from other Arcanum laws.

Of course, any use of the Divine Mirror for any purpose other than entertainment was strictly prohibited. If abuse of this power were discovered, the offender would be banished to Tenkai, the upper world of the heavens.

Also, once a Divine Mirror was activated, any nearby god or goddess could observe what was going on by activating their own mirror. It was extremely risky for any god or goddess to use this ability for their own gain. None of them had been that foolish.

However, this particular goddess had a way to "convince" male gods to allow her to use this ability: her beauty.

"Just for today." "It won't cause any problems for any other *Familia*." "One room in the Dungeon." These were the conditions of her contract. She had accepted the risk and opened the mirror.

This was all to make sure she saw the battle with her own eyes.

"…Ahh!"

Freya's expression shifted from surprise, to joy, then enchantment at the scene unfolding in front of her.

"Ha-ha, ha-h-aha…?! Can you see this, Ottar? Can you see the beauty…?!"

It was shining.

Bell's spirit shone through.

Bright enough to burn his image in Freya's eyes.

Despite being so radiant, the light from his soul was still clear.

A pure wish.

He was pure, no hidden agenda and completely clean. The boy only had one thing on his mind.

Unlimited possibilities were blooming within Bell.

The battle raged on.

Bell and the Minotaur exchanged blows rhythmically, each jockeying for better position.

Two sets of legs dug into the grass, spun, kicked, and dodged.

Neither of them stopped moving.

Don't worry about its size.

Bell looked up at the monster with a strong calm in his eyes and ice in his veins.

The fear that had consumed him before was gone.

Free from the despair that bound him, Bell had no intention of retreating.

He engaged the Minotaur's attacks without hesitation, his new-found courage guiding him past each blow.

It's big, that's all! Keep your eyes open!

His mind was in complete control; his eyes did what they were told.

Indeed, the Minotaur possessed amazing strength. If Bell took a direct shot, his very bones would shatter under the force of impact. That's what Minotaurs were known for: being strong enough to kill in one shot.

But that was all.

No matter how strong the attack, it had to hit its target first. Even the cleaver in its right hand was nothing more than a slab of metal if it couldn't connect.

Bell's eyes saw things more clearly than ever before.

His ruby-red eyes were sharp enough to see everything, from the Minotaur's expression to the movements of its muscles.

As long as he stayed calm, this information told him everything he needed to know. The beast put all of its strength into every attack, muscles bulging menacingly under its skin. However, this not only told Bell the timing of each attack but the direction as well.

The Minotaur's movements were straightforward, uncomplicated.

The beast's attacks were so obvious that Bell could predict them easily.

I fought an opponent hundreds of times faster than this thing!

Compared to the girl who trained him, his current opponent might as well have been a tree in the wind.

Even the fact it was wielding an adventurer's weapon just meant it had learned how to use a sword, nothing more.

If he couldn't handle something like this, he had no chance of catching up to *her*.

The Minotaur's attacks would not connect. He wouldn't let them.

Each swing of its massive sword hit nothing but empty air. Bell used his jet-black knife to guide each strike into the ground.

Speed had become his trump card. He used every bit of it to dodge, evade, and defend against every attack.

"...The heck's up with that knife? Blockin' something that big with nothin' more than a tooth pick?"

"No, something more than just the knife..."

"Impressive. He's using technique against the Minotaur's attacks."

A burst of violet light, and the cleaver was thrown backward with a metallic echo.

The words rolled out of Bete's mouth as he watched the battle. Reveria and Fynn answered him.

While the Hestia Knife was special in that it improved along with the user's Status, there was no way it could take the nearly two-meder cleaver head-on. Add the Minotaur's brute strength to the attack, and it had no chance.

Therefore, Bell was aiming for the side of the blade.

The impact of Bell's knife created just enough space for his body to slide past the Minotaur's attacks. It was a keen strategy, but there was absolutely no room for error.

It was a technique he "borrowed" from Aiz. However, every second and every movement determined life or death.

Every one of the girl's teachings that had been pounded into his body now put Bell on equal footing with the Minotaur.

Everything he had learned on top of the city wall was being put to use in this one battle.

"He really is good at dodging. But..."

"The boy can't finish it off."

The Amazonian sisters watched, Tione with a distant look in her eyes and Tiona nervously shaking, as Bell intercepted the cleaver with his knife and went for a counterattack with the baselard in his left hand. But it wasn't enough.

The short sword had succeeded in cutting the Minotaur a few times, but the wounds were not deep enough to inflict any damage. They were nothing more than scratches on the surface.

The Minotaur's breath was ragged as it lined up another shot at Bell.

"...Minotaurs are hard to cut."

The Kenki gave her opinion on Minotaurs. Considering she had taken down hundreds of thousands of monsters, her words carried a lot of weight.

The bulging muscles all over the beast's body were not just for decoration. Of course they were visual evidence of the monster's overall strength, but their density made them feel like rubber.

In addition, Minotaur skin was an extremely valuable drop item used to create armor with very high Defense. Even if an attack was strong enough to pierce the skin, there was a very real chance the blade would get stuck in the muscles. Only a strong direct attack had any chance of slaying a Minotaur.

The Minotaur was one of the few monsters that had broken away from groups. It could do this because its Defense was so high. When adventurers thought about the area of the Dungeon known as the Middle Fortress, the Minotaur was always first to come to mind.

"MROOOOOOAH!"

"GEH!"

Little by little, Bell was starting to turn the tables against the monster that exemplified attack and defense.

The Minotaur was categorized as a Level-Two monster. Being at only Level One, Bell was in a hole that should be impossible to overcome.

That was the Minotaur's distinct advantage.

For Bell, this was a wall of despair.

The Status the Minotaur was born with should have been strong enough to overcome any techniques Bell could throw at it.

"Mr. Bell…"

Lilly had recovered enough to stand on her own two feet, but it took a large amount of effort to squeeze Bell's name out of her lungs.

She joined the line of onlookers as Bell yet again guided the monster's cleaver just past his face and into the dirt.

Not losing a beat, the Minotaur used its forward momentum to launch a powerful kick toward Bell's chest. However, Bell saw it coming and used his agility to get out of the way and bring the Hestia Knife forward.

The Minotaur flung the cleaver in front of the knife. Another sharp metallic echo filled the room.

"……!"

"MROOOOOOOOOOOOOOOOOO!!"

Bell couldn't hide his surprise at the Minotaur's reaction. It was almost as though the beast was scared of the Hestia Knife.

Without a doubt, the Minotaur realized that this knife was the only legitimate threat that Bell presented.

Bell had reached the same conclusion.

His enemy, the Minotaur, only let its guard down the moment Bell's knife was no longer in position to counterattack.

If the blade could pierce the muscle, the Minotaur's bones were in danger. The beast understood.

As Bell stared into its eyes, sensing its unnatural intelligence and looking at its broken horn, Bell knew what he had to do.

"EAT THIS!!"

Jumping back to get space, Bell cleared his mind.

Almost as if signaling "stay back," he thrust his right arm forward.

The Minotaur's eyes went wide for an instant before—

"FIREBOLT!!"

An electric inferno thundered forward.

Amid explosions and crackles of burning lightning, the beast was forced backward.

The Minotaur let out a ferocious roar that echoed off the ceiling from behind the smoke and flames.

"...Was there a spell? That was Magic."

"No...Didn't even see 'im chant words."

What allowed Level-One Bell to take on a category Level-Two monster like the Minotaur was Magic.

Even though Bell could be physically overpowered, his ticket out of certain death was without a doubt his Swift-Strike Magic, Firebolt.

Unfortunately—

"UuWWWAAAOOOOOOOOOOOOOOOOOOOOOOOO!!"

"......!"

—it didn't work.

"Too weak."

"Ahh, that won't end it."

"The activation speed was very impressive, but his opponent is too strong. Under the right circumstances, a spell like that could be extremely useful..."

The flaw in Bell's Magic had been revealed.

It didn't have enough power.

There were injuries and burns all over the Minotaur's two-meder-tall body. However, there was nothing more. Its skin had not been pierced deep enough.

Normal offensive spells might have been able to, but Bell's Firebolt was not yet strong enough to deliver a killing blow to the Minotaur.

It didn't have enough power.

"Out of options?"

"It's too early to call this match...is what I'd like to say."

A new wave of rage engulfed the Minotaur as Bell once again charged forward to engage it in combat.

Reveria and Fynn appraised the battle realistically as Bell's assault on the Minotaur grew longer and longer.

No matter how long Bell could hold his ground against the Mino-taur, he had no chance of winning unless his attacks inflicted dam-age on the beast. Even going for the one-hit kill by piercing its chest was doomed to fail. Bell's knife was not long enough to reach the magic stone inside.

His only viable option now was to accept death and try to take it down with him.

Once Bell made that decision, there was a 99-percent chance that the Minotaur would win.

Attacks were meaningless. That signaled failure in any battle.

The Minotaur roared again.

Yet another full-power swing from overhead and Bell moved to evade. But this time he was too slow. While his body got out of the way, the baselard was hit and split in two on impact.

Bell's face went hard as a rock.

"Now the boy has no weapon."

Fynn's voice rode a soft breeze throughout the room.

The Minotaur's ferocious swing continued past Bell and into the floor, making a small crater in the process.

Bell flung his right arm in front of his face, what was left of his short sword still clutched in his fist. Debris bouncing off his body, Bell was thrown back by the sheer force of the blow.

Bell was airborne for mere moments before landing and looking back at his opponent.

—*No weapon? There's one right here!*

His eyes looking just over his right elbow, Bell locked onto the Minotaur's cleaver. Taking a step forward, he threw his own broken sword at the beast with all of his might.

"UOO?!"

Bell's surprise attack caught the Minotaur off guard.

The reflection of the oncoming weapon grew in the Minotaur's eyes, light glancing off the broken blade as it spun.

At this rate, the broken baselard would hit the Minotaur right between the eyes. The monster quickly jerked its neck to the side. The cutting edge made contact with the Minotaur's cheek; a drip of blood rolled down its face.

As for Bell—

He didn't wait to see where his sneak attack landed; he'd already launched his next plan.

"—?!"

"YEEEEEAAAA!!!"

The diversion had cost the Minotaur valuable seconds, and it was slow to react.

Bell's body was twisted, lining up the Hestia Knife for a strike with his right arm hidden behind his back.

The Minotaur had been trained very well. Eyes focused, its put the cleaver between itself and the oncoming human, directly in the path of Bell's oncoming attack.

Forcing the massive sword out of the ground, it used the flat part of the blade as a shield against the Hestia Knife.

It worked!

A shred of surprise swept over the Minotaur's face when its eyes caught something unexpected.

The blade that was hidden behind Bell's shoulder was not black.

A white blade; an ordinary dagger.

Bell had switched the Hestia Knife to his left hand the moment he threw the baselard.

He pulled the dagger back, and brought his left arm out of the shadows.

His ruby-red eyes were not keyed onto the Minotaur, but on the cleaver.

"HEH!!"

"GUWAAOO?!"

Holding the Hestia Knife so the blade came out of the bottom of his hand, Bell's upward swing connected with the Minotaur's right hand.

While the Minotaur had managed to get the blade into position, its stance was weak. Knocked off balance from Bell's charge, the cleaver was useless in defense.

SHINK! The knife buried itself into the Minotaur's right hand, cutting flesh, bone and tendons alike.

Amid the beast's screams of pain, Bell used his momentum to spin the knife and kick the flat part of the massive cleaver. The monstrous sword went airborne with the Minotaur's fingers still attached.

Fynn and the others watched as blood sprayed from the Minotaur's injured hand.

"MAAAWWOOOOOOOOOOOOOOOOO?!"

The beast reeled backward and grabbed its wrist in pain.

Ignoring the blast coming from the Minotaur's throat, Bell crouched down before springing forward.

Using the beast's body like a ladder, the boy jumped up to eye level with the Minotaur. One last kick to it shoulder, and Bell flipped backward, carving an arc in the air.

But this was no ordinary attack. Bell's thin body was aimed directly for the blood-splattered cleaver lying on the ground.

Whoosh-whoosh. Bell landed on his hands just short of the blade. A heartbeat later, he grabbed it.

A quick roll and he was up again.

"M-MOOOOOOAAAAAAAAAAAAAAAAAAAAAAAAAA?!"

Fighting back the pain in its arm, the Minotaur turned around to find Bell, and immediately charged forward.

Its left arm thrust forward, it howled as if to say, "Give that back!" The Minotaur wasn't about to give up its weapon so easily.

Bell stood with his back to the beast, the hilt of the cleaver clutched in his left hand as he turned around and raised his right arm.

"FIREBOLT!"

An explosion ensued.

"————Mo-oo?!"

The Minotaur's feet left the ground after getting hit by the Magic at this close range.

Just as it had before, the speed and power of Bell's Magic pushed the Minotaur back. But this time, the beast flew backward with its feet floundering in the air.

The sudden web of burning lightning ensnared the Minotaur, sending pieces of singed fur falling to the ground. But the beast got its footing and pushed through the cloud of smoke rising around it. Violet sparks of lightning ignited the grass, creating a ring of small flames and pyres of smoke around the battle.

Before anyone could blink—

It was Bell who emerged from the smoke, carrying the cleaver in both hands.

"HYYYYYAAAAAAAAAAAHHHHHHHHHHHHHHHHHH HHH!!"

He hoisted the massive weapon above his head and brought it down with all his might.

"UWAAOooo?!"

A thick red line appeared on the Minotaur's chest, cutting through flesh that was thick as armor.

"That hit?!"

Blood sprayed out of the diagonal cut that started at the shoulder and ended just below the beast's rib cage. The singed grass beneath was splattered with the dark liquid.

Words of surprise escaped Tiona's mouth before she realized it. The Minotaur stumbled backward yet again.

Bell wasn't about to let this chance slip by.

"TAKE THHHHIIIIIISSSSSSSSSSSSSSSSSSSSSSSSSSSSSS!!"

"Muwoo?!"

Bell charged the Minotaur, using its own blade against it.

The boy unleashed all the destructive power contained in his arms as the massive blade cut through the air itself.

Thrusting his heels into the ground, he brought the blade crashing down.

He missed his colossal target, but the Minotaur had no time to rest. The next attack was already coming.

"Heh, the kid sucks…!"

"But he is pushing it back."

It was safe to say that large blades were not Bell's strong suit.

It looked more like the blade was swinging *him* around. In a different situation, it would have been a very comical picture: a thin boy trying to wield a blade twice his size and losing.

However, his vigorous assault had the Minotaur on the ropes.

He had become a bladed tornado. Flashes of brilliant silver surrounded him as Bell's constant screams echoed throughout the room.

The bull-monster was visibly shaking. Still in shock from this drastic turn of events, it wasn't able to mount a defense. Its only hope was to dodge the onslaught.

While the Minotaur managed to avoid a direct shot, more thick red lines crisscrossed its arms and legs. Even more of its blood splashed onto the ground following streaks of silver light.

Where Bell's short sword had failed so many times, the cleaver was inflicting actual damage at an incredible rate.

"Mmoooh—MWWAAAOOOOOOOOOOOOOOOOOOOOO OOO!!!"

The Minotaur howled in an attempt to instill fear.

The beast's instincts had awakened. Eyes narrowed and teeth bared, it was as if the beast were screaming, "DON'T GET COCKY!"

Driving its heels into the dirt, the Minotaur punched the blade out of the way and charged forward.

"—!!"

The last round.

The two combatants locked eyes, each howling sounds that had lost all meaning.

The Minotaur menacingly flexed its muscles. The human responded by swinging the sword above his head. This battle would come down to swordsmanship and technique versus primal strength and power.

The two charged and collided, going blow for blow, one step forward, one step back. Neither showed signs of slowing down.

The Minotaur threw an off-balance kick toward Bell's face, but was blocked by the sword.

Bell used the sword to swing himself up and land a punch just beneath the Minotaur's eye.

The impact cracked bones in his hand, but he flew past the Minotaur, landing just behind.

The battle raged on. Hoof-shaped imprints in the grass; slices of dirt missing after the deep impacts of the cleaver; even the lights above began to dim. The stage of their battle was breaking.

Each blow was thrown at full strength with the intent to kill. Neither combatant was going to pull any punches now.

Can't stop, won't stop, can't give ground.

Blood-splattered silver sword met horn; sparks flew. Bell spun and struck again.

Everyone watching the battle taking place on the lower-ninth floor of the Dungeon knew the end was near.

"YYYYYAAAAAAAAAH!!!"

"UGOOUU?!"

Bell ducked under the Minotaur's punch and turned, using every muscle in his body. The cleaver connected with the Minotaur's exposed side, digging deep into its gut.

However, the blade stopped as it hit abdominal muscles that were as hard as rocks. The force of the collision threw the Minotaur to the side and withdrew the blade in one solid motion.

Crack. Bell thought he heard a strange noise come from the cleaver, but it was quickly drowned out by the Minotaur's screams of agony.

"FOOHH, FOOHH, UWWAOOOOOOOOOOOOOOOO!!"

There were five meders between the two combatants.

The Minotaur squeezed its wound shut, eyes bloodshot and fuming. Taking in a deep breath, it thrust its hands into the ground.

Despite being hands, the beast's appendages were so badly damaged that they looked more like hooves. With all four limbs on the ground, it lowered its head. Its hindquarters up high, the Minotaur had become in essence a raging bull.

Bete and every one of his compatriots stood silently, completely focused on the battle.

The Minotaur had been pushed all the way into the corner of the room, and its only way out was to charge through Bell.

It still had its trump card: the sharp horn on top of its head. And it was aimed right at Bell's heart.

The Minotaur was preparing to unleash a rush powerful enough to obliterate anything in its way.

However at this distance, it wouldn't be able to build up enough speed. It could hope for half power at best.

The fact that it was this desperate was proof of just how much it had been driven back.

"—"

The Minotaur's eyes glinted as its last shred of pride, the one compete horn on its head, took aim.

The utmost concentration shot out of the deepest part of the combatant's eyes. It was an unspoken understanding. Two wills were about to clash.

Each took in one last breath and for a moment an eerie stillness filled the air.

Bell's gaze met the Minotaur's glare.

And then...

"HYYYYYAAAAAAAAAAAAAAAAAAAAHHHHHHHHH HHHHHH!!!!"

"UUUWWWWAAAAOOOOOOOOOOOOOOOOOOOOO OOO!!!"

They collided.

—*Naïve.*

Reveria almost looked away as the combatants charged head-on.

"Idiot!"

"No, Mr. Bell!"

The voices of Bete and the others rang out, punctuated by Lilly's screams.

Their cries rode the shock wave of impact, reaching Bell's and the Minotaur's ears as nothing more than part of the hurricane of sound engulfing them.

In that moment, all eyes shot open as each poured every ounce of power into one spot. Their skins burned with a desire for victory.

A downward strike and an upward thrust.

Both hit head-on at full force.

In that moment, the battle turned yet again.

"—"

A metallic crack rang out.

A web of cracks ran down the cleaver's blade from the point of impact with the Minotaur's horn.

"UUWWOOOO!!"

The weapon shattered.

Just as *Loki Familia* found out on their last expedition, all weapons would eventually become useless without repair.

And this heavily neglected blade had reached its breaking point.

It had been trapped in the Dungeon for almost a week.

The cleaver had survived Ottar's training, as well as taken countless lives at the hands of the Minotaur. It just couldn't take any more punishment.

The impact broke the blade just above the hilt, shattering the base and sending the rest of the weapon flying into parts unknown.

On the other hand, there wasn't even a scratch on the Minotaur's horn.

A rain of silver shards clouded Bell's vision.

Bell followed through with his attack angled to the right, the scrap metal in his hands passing harmlessly by the Minotaur's face.

The Minotaur's attack had been a leftward thrust. The combatants slid cleanly past each other, no damage inflicted.

The two locked eyes for a moment. Bell caught a glimpse of the smirk on the Minotaur's face.

It was not a ridiculing smile of a sore winner, but a burly smile of someone desperate for victory.

The Minotaur could see its chance at triumph, now that its opponent had lost his last trump card.

Bell was silent for an instant, white hair covering his ruby-red eyes in shadow.

The beast flew past his line of sight, almost as though in slow motion.

My trump card—

Bell...

—is right here!!

...drew a jet-black knife from its sheath.

"!!"

Bell slammed on the brakes.

He came to a sudden halt behind the Minotaur's ferocious rush.

Ignoring the screams of agony erupting from his knees, Bell turned around.

The two had been back to back. However, Bell's Agility had gone beyond normal limits. His second ace in the hole opened a new window for attack.

The blade sticking out beneath Bell's fingers in his right hand, the Hestia Knife carved a brilliant violet arc through the air.

The Minotaur had come to a stop as well, its head still tilted left and the light emitting from Bell's blade reflecting off its eye.

"SHAAA!!"

"UWOA?!"

The Hestia Knife plunged into the Minotaur's exposed right flank, piercing its defenses.

Power, momentum, and centrifugal force combined into one spot. The impact of Bell's sudden sneak attack shook the Minotaur to its core and sent its body listing to the side.

Bell drove the knife as deep as it would go with all of his might before yelling:

"FIREBOLT!!!"

BOOM! A shock wave rocked the Minotaur's body.

The beast's chest expanded suddenly, as if something deep within had exploded.

Scarlet flames erupted from the wound made by the Hestia Knife. The Minotaur's bloodshot eyes opened as wide as they would go.

"FIREBOLTTT!!!"

One more blast.

As strange as it seemed to the onlookers, the Minotaur's upper body swayed like sails on a boat.

No matter how thick its muscles, nor how resistant its skin was to Magic, its insides were a different story.

Bell's Magic drove the knife even deeper still, a web of flames burning the Minotaur from within.

The flaming electric current searched for a way out and suddenly found the beast's throat.

"GEGAHH!" Scarlet flames erupted from its nose and mouth.

"GAHA, GEHAH……GUWAAOOOOOOOOO?!"

Its throat and mouth being burned to ashes, it put all of its remaining power into its elbow and thrust it backward at Bell.

A rejection of the utmost strength.

This attack, even without aiming, would undoubtedly turn Bell's body into a pile of meat.

Death would come a moment later.

And then at the very moment the hammer made contact with the skin of Bell's head—

Bell was faster.

"FFFIIIIIIRRRRRRREEEEEEEBOOOOOOOOOLLLLLLLLLTTTTT TTTT!!!!!!!!!"

Another burst.

"_____?!"

A blinding flash of light—and the Minotaur's upper body burst into pieces.

More explosions filled the room as flames overtook the still-intact remains of the beast.

Scarlet sparks had reached as high as the ceiling, smoke covering them moments later. Bete and the others gazed at the carnage and thought it looked more like a volcanic eruption than the climax of a duel. The Minotaur's legs, which had mostly survived the blast in one piece, remained upright for a heartbeat before collapsing to the ground.

Next came a rain of charred flesh and blood.

The rising smoke colored each of the thousands of fragments as they passed through and eventually hit the ground.

Amid the sounds of the remaining pieces showering the ground, a single magic stone fell from the ceiling. It spun over and over before hitting the ground with a sharp smack.

"Did he finish it...?"

Bete whispered in a state of shock.

He couldn't take his eyes off Bell, unable to believe what he'd just seen.

Bell had his back to *Loki Familia*, but Bete's question was only aimed at himself.

Bete wondered how long ago it was that he himself had became strong enough to take down a Minotaur.

No, how long had it taken him to become strong enough to take one down alone?

These questions ignited a fire within him, his face turning red.

What started as irritation flaring up in his gut turned into full-blown embarrassment. It spread to every corner of his body.

"...Mind Down."

"He...he's standing there, out cold..."

The Amazonian sisters stood there in shock. Their voices couldn't hide their disbelief as they looked at Bell, frozen in his last attack position. His right arm was still in front of his body, his hand curled as if holding the Hestia Knife.

The girls were in awe at the boy who'd spent every last drop of energy to win the battle.

It was as if a book were open in front of them, the hero of the story jumping out of the pages.

"...! Answer me, prum! Just what the hell is that kid...?!"

"Mr. Bell...Mr. Bell!!"

"Hey, I'm talkin' to you...Tsk!"

Bete snapped his tongue at the girl as she ran toward Bell on unsteady feet.

The wolf man watched her go, tormented by feelings he couldn't understand.

Then he noticed the state of Bell's back. Armor long since broken, his black inner shirt had been torn to shreds. His shoulder blades

were completely exposed, only a few threads of fabric kept the shirt on his back.

What's more, hieroglyphs were visible just beneath the damaged cloth.

"—! Reveria! Tell me the kid's Status—now!"

"...Are you telling me to steal personal information?"

Only the skin on Bell's upper back was visible.

The slots containing his Magic and Skills were obscured by what was left of his shirt. Despite all the holes, most of Bell's Status remained hidden.

"It's not freakin' stealin' when it's that wide-open. Fine, if ya ain't gonna look I'll ask someone who will. I can't be the only one that wants answers."

Bete felt it wasn't against the law if the information just happened to come into your line of sight. He fumed at Reveria, for she had the eyes to see at this distance and the knowledge to decipher the hieroglyphs.

The knowledgeable elf sighed and cast her gaze toward Bell. Perhaps she, too, was interested.

Her dark emerald eyes found the hieroglyphs on Bell's back.

"Dammit, what's takin' ya so long?"

"Be patient, I've almost finished—"

Reveria suddenly stopped talking, her words trailing off.

Bete glared at her. Tiona and the others drifted toward the elf, drawn in by curiosity.

A moment later, the elf let out an uneven laugh.

"...Heh. Ha-ha-ha-ha-ha."

"The heck's wrong with ya, hey?! Son of a...Yo, Aiz. Ya can read hieroglyphs, too, right? Can ya see anythin' from there?"

Bete angrily bared his fangs at Reveria. It looked as though something had popped loose in her head, her shoulders shaking as she laughed. So, Bete directed his question a few meders ahead where Aiz was standing.

The human girl was still rooted to the same spot, her eyes focused only on the boy. She gave a quick nod and looked at his back.

Her golden gaze honed in on their target with the precision of a blade.

"...S."

"...Huh?"

"All of his abilities are S."

"ALL S?!"

Bete's voice joined Tiona's and the others' in surprise. All other words had left them.

In reality, Aiz couldn't see Bell's Magic level due to what remained of his inner shirt. However, considering what had just transpired she had a feeling it was close enough.

There was one other fact she hadn't told Bete and the others.

It was the very thing that had sent Reveria for a loop. SS. The boy possessed an ability that went beyond normal limits. It made her eyes spin.

"His name?"

A new sound echoed.

A voice cut through the stunned silence.

Everyone except Aiz turned around to find the source.

With the eyes of his compatriots on him, Fynn slowly walked forward while tapping the shaft of his spear on his shoulder.

He eyed the human with a calm gaze as he came up to meet the rest of his battle party. Asking his question again, the prum had a more serious look on his face.

"What is the boy's name?"

"Hell if I know...Haven't heard it."

"...Reveria. Please stop laughing like that."

"Hee-hee...Ahh, my apologies. What were you asking?"

"Please check the boy's Status for his name. I'd like to know."

"Yes, that would be good to know. Please wait a moment..."

The Status worked like a contract between a god and the being who received their falna—their blessing.

To make the contract binding, the god engraved their seal next to the recipient's real name.

Reveria squinted her eyes in an effort to read the boy's name. But before she could open her mouth, another voice beat her to it.

It was Aiz.

"Bell."

"Aiz…"

Her soft voice cut through the air.

She hadn't budged an inch.

She didn't even turn to face Tiona when the Amazonian girl responded. Her eyes were planted firmly on Bell.

"Bell Cranell."

They could see the boy's reflection clearly in her golden eyes.

Period of Employment: one month

Total Monsters Slain: 3,001

Three days ago, he became by far the fastest adventurer on record to reach Level Two.

EPILOGUE **PAGE 0 → PAGE 1**

I hear someone crying.

A small child, tears pouring down his face, hiccupping over and over and clinging to a large chest.

And holding onto the child covered in blood and dirt, patting him lightly on the head, is one old man.

"Does it hurt, Bell?"

The boy listens to the soft voice overhead and is about to nod, but quickly shakes his head no. He starts to cry again.

The old man smiles and continues to embrace the trembling boy, comforting him.

"I told you not to go outside the village, now didn't I? Those goblins did quite a number on you."

That voice, this grass, that smile...I know this place.

The setting sun, a face that I thought I would never see again, everything is so bright.

"But you did well. You didn't give in to those monsters. Be proud."

The sky is filled with brilliant shades of red, fields of golden wheat dancing in the evening breeze.

Amid this beautiful scenery from my memory, an old man's kind words make their way into the heart of the young boy.

All of this will no doubt be lost in a deep corner of his memory.

Once he wakes up, it will seem like an old, far-off wish.

An irreplaceable longing from childhood.

"You looked good out there, Bell."

Seeing the old man smile, the boy starts bawling yet again.

Yet, inside his hazy, tear-filled eyes, there is a glimmer of admiration.

Looking at the man's face that is so close to his own, the boy fights back his tears and swears to himself.

As the child's lips move, I feel my own and move with him. Our voices overlap, becoming one.

I want to become someone like you.

Like the one who saved me, someone strong like you.

Someone like my hero, I want to be like you.

"Is that all? Too low, too low. An old geezer like me your goal? You should aim higher."

Well then, I'll become one of those heroes from the stories.

One of those heroes whom everyone praises.

Will you say that you like me?

Will you say that you're proud of me?

Will you be happy?

"Oh yes, I'll smile so hard my cheeks will fall off. I'll brag to anyone and everyone that you're my grandson. I'll tell them in a big voice you make me proud."

Okay, then. If you're willing to say that. For sure I'll…

You'll always watch over me from heaven, my one and only…

"I'll always be watching. You'll always be on my mind. So don't do anything for my sake."

The old man laughs again, wrinkles appearing all over his happy face.

"Real men chase after the ladies. Dash after them at full speed. Puff your chest out. Head up, facing forward."

Then the old man looks down, a serious look in his eyes as he says:

"If it's for the love of a woman, you can become a hero, or anything you want. You can do anything."

The last golden light of the setting sun grows dim.

I reach out desperately into the growing darkness. That's when I hear him say these words:

"You are, after all, *my* grandson."

"What are you dreaming about, Bell…" whispered Hestia as she watched a tear work its way down Bell's cheek.

A member of her family lay sleeping in a bed inside the medical center within Babel Tower. He had been carried here by the blond girl with golden eyes. His supporter was with them as well. The only sound in their quiet little room was Bell's peaceful breathing.

The boy, who had just overcome the most intense battle of his life, wore no expression in sleep, just peaceful calm.

"...And there are so many things I have to tell you, but..."

Hestia gently wiped away the tear that came out of Bell's closed eye.

Bell's mouth was slightly open, his breathing deep and steady. Hestia couldn't help but smile.

"You did your best, didn't you...Congratulations."

She looked around the room once before leaning forward and brushing Bell's bangs upward. She pressed her lips to his forehead.

The goddess blushed softly as she read the story engraved in the boy's back, her eyes slowly closing.

"This is the first page."

【BELL・CRANELL】

BELONGS TO: HESTIA FAMILIA
RACE: HUMAN
JOB: ADVENTURER
DUNGEON RANGE: LOWER TENTH FLOOR
WEAPONS: HESTIA KNIFE, DAGGER
CURRENT WORTH: 79,500 VALS

STATUS

Lv. **1**

STRENGTH: S 982   DEFENSE: S 900   UTILITY: S 988
AGILITY: SS1049   MAGIC: B 751

《MAGIC》

【FIREBOLT】

• SWIFT STRIKE MAGIC

《SKILL》

【 REALIS PHRASE 】

• RAPID GROWTH
• CONTINUED DESIRE RESULTS IN CONTINUED GROWTH
• STRONGER DESIRE RESULTS IN STRONGER GROWTH

《SCHWEIZERDEGEN》

• BASELARD.
• ONCE DECORATED THE WALLS OF A GNOME SHOP. 19,000 VALS.
• A MASTERWORK. MORE THAN GOOD ENOUGH FOR BEGINNING ADVENTURERS.
• BELL ORIGINALLY RECEIVED IT FROM A DISHONEST PRUM AS A PARTING PRESENT. AT A DISCOUNT, OF COURSE.

Afterword

Part one is complete.

While there were a few bumps along the way, I feel like I've written exactly what I wanted to read and write for the third installment of the series.

Throughout writing this book, I have come to realize that those who go on adventures usually win in the end.

Venturing into the unknown requires a great deal of courage. In my personal opinion, going somewhere where you know absolutely nothing is very scary.

That being said, the moment you take your first step toward a place where you don't know what is going to happen, something changes inside of you.

Other authors have said this before, but I agree: No one can prove they have overcome their challenges, only that they have grown in the process.

Successes and failures stick with us for our lifetime. However, those who face obstacles without compromising who they are will grow. Of that, I'm sure.

Go on an adventure.

Strive to be an adventurer.

While it's in my nature to do an about-face at the last moment, I am always trying to do something new.

And now to show my gratitude.

Completing the story and getting it into print is thanks to a great number of people. I would like to extend a special thank-you to Suzuhito Yasuda, H2SO4, Kurogin, Fox Mark, Siki Douji, toi8, Yuuji Nimura, Kiyoshi Haimura, and Ruroo for your beautiful artwork, as well as everyone involved in making this book a reality.

Also, thank you to every person who has read this series from volume one. I am extremely thankful for your support.

Next, I hope to steadily expand the scope of this world, starting in the next volume. It is my goal to continually improve the series, and I will do my best to deliver a high-quality volume four as soon as possible.

Let's meet again in those pages.

Thank you from the bottom of my heart. Until next time.

Fujino Omori

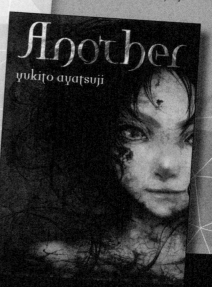